em

em

Kim Thúy

TRANSLATED FROM THE FRENCH
BY SHEILA FISCHMAN

SEVEN STORIES PRESS
New York • Oakland

Published by arrangement with Groupe Librex, Montréal, Quebec, Canada

Seven Stories Press
140 Watts Street
New York, NY 10013
www.sevenstories.com

College professors and high school and middle school teachers
may order free examination copies of Seven Stories Press titles.
viisit https://www.sevenstories.com/pg/resources-academics
or email academics@sevenstories.com..

Library of Congress Cataloging-in-Publication Data

Names: Thúy, Kim, author. | Fischman, Sheila, translator.
Title: Em / Kim Thúy ; translated from the French by Sheila Fischman.
Other titles: Em. English
Description: New York : Seven Stories Press, [2021]
Identifiers: LCCN 2021032738 (print) | LCCN 2021032739 (ebook) | ISBN 9781644211151 (hardcover) | ISBN 9781644211168 (ebook)
Subjects: LCGFT: Novels.
Classification: LCC PQ3919.3.T48 E413 2021 (print) | LCC PQ3919.3.T48 (ebook) | DDC 843/.92--dc23
LC record available at https://lccn.loc.gov/2021032738
LC ebook record available at https://lccn.loc.gov/2021032739

The translation of this book was assisted by a grant from the government of Quebec (SODEC).

Text design: Jennifer Griffiths
Image credits: Louis Boudreault (page 126)

Printed in the USA.

For the forgotten and the unnamed

—KIM THÚY

For Don

again

always

—SHEILA FISCHMAN

The word *em* refers to
the little brother or little sister in a family;
or the younger of two friends;
or the woman in a couple.
I like to think that the word *em* is the homonym
of the verb *aimer*, "to love," in French,
in the imperative: *aime*.

A genesis of truth

War, again. In every conflict zone, good steals in and 1
edges its way right into the cracks of evil. Treason complements heroism, love flirts with abandonment. The enemies advance towards one another, all with the same goal: to triumph. In this shared exercise, what is human shows itself to be at once strong, mad, cowardly, great, crude, innocent, ignorant, devout, cruel, courageous . . . That is the reason for war. Again.

I'm going to tell you the truth, some true stories at least, but only partially, incompletely, more or less. Because it's impossible for me to re-create the blue nuances in the sky just as Rob, the marine, was reading a letter from his lover, while at the same time the rebel, Vinh, was writing to his own love during a brief lull, a moment of deceptive calm. Was it a Mayan and azure blue, or a French and cerulean blue? When Private John discovered the list of insurgents hidden in a pot of manioc flour, how many kilos were there? Had the flour just been milled?

What was the temperature of the water when Monsieur Út was thrown into the well before being burned alive by Sergeant Peter's flame-thrower? Did Monsieur Út weigh half as much as Peter, or two-thirds? Was it the itching of his mosquito bites that so unsettled Peter?

For nights at a time, I tried to imagine Travis's walk, Hoa's shyness, Nick's fear, Tuân's despair, the bullet wounds of some and the victories of others in the forest, in the city, in the rain, in the mud. Every night, to the rhythm of ice cubes dropping into their container in the freezer, my research assaulted me with the knowledge that my imagination would never be able to grasp the whole reality. In one testimony, a soldier remembers seeing the enemy running full speed towards a tank, carrying on his shoulder an M67 rifle, 1.3 metres long and weighing seventeen kilos. Facing that soldier was a man ready to die in order to kill his enemies, ready to kill while dying, ready to let death triumph. How to imagine such selflessness, such unconditional commitment to a cause?

How to contemplate that a woman might carry her two small children into the jungle over hundreds of kilometres, tying the first to a branch in order to protect him from wild animals while she moved off with the second, tied him up in turn, and went back to the first child to repeat the journey with him? Yet this woman described her trek to me in her ninety-two-year-old combatant's voice. Despite our six hours of conversation, there are still a thousand details I lack. I forgot to ask her where she got the ropes, and if her sons still bear marks on their bodies from being tied up. Who knows if these memories have not been erased to leave behind only one, the taste of wild tubers she chewed into mush to feed to her children? Who knows . . .

If your heart shudders on reading these stories of foreseeable madness, unimagined love, or everyday heroism, know that the whole truth would very probably have provoked in you either respiratory failure or euphoria. In this book, truth is fragmented, incomplete, unfinished, in both time and space. Then is it still the truth? I'll let you reply in a way that relates to your own story, your own truth. Meanwhile, I promise you in the words that follow a certain ordering of the emotions, along with feelings whose disarray cannot be denied.

RUBBER

4 White gold flows from wounds inflicted on rubber trees. For centuries, the Maya, the Aztecs, the peoples of the Amazon, collected this liquid and used it to make shoes, waterproof fabric, and rubber balls. When European explorers discovered this material, they first used it to manufacture elastic that would hold up their garters. At the dawn of the twentieth century, the demand increased at the meteoric speed with which automobiles multiplied, transforming the landscape. The need then became so great and so demanding that synthetic latex, a material that meets seventy percent of our current needs, had to be produced. Despite all the efforts made in laboratories, only pure latex, whose name of *caoutchouc* in French means "the tears (*caa*) of the tree (*ochu*)," can withstand the acceleration, the pressure, and the thermal range imposed on airplane tires and the joints in a space shuttle. The more humanity succeeds in accelerating its rhythm, the more it requires a latex produced naturally,

at the speed of Earth's rotation around the sun, in accord with lunar eclipses.

Thanks to its elasticity, its resistance, and its impermeability, natural latex swathes our extremities like a second skin in order to protect us from the consequences of desire. During the Franco-Prussian War in 1870 and the following year, the rate of infections contracted sexually by the troops grew from less than four percent to more than seventy-five percent, which later led, during the First World War, to the German government's giving high priority to the production of condoms to protect its soldiers, even though there was a serious shortage of rubber.

Certainly, bullets kill, but so, perhaps, does desire.

Alexandre

6 Alexandre was well acquainted with the discipline he needed to impose on his six thousand ragged Vietnamese coolies. His workers knew better than he did how to plant a hatchet into the trunk of a rubber tree, at an angle of forty-five degrees to the vertical, to make the first tears ooze. They were faster than he was at positioning the coconut shell bowls that would collect the drops of latex accumulating at the bottom of the wound. Alexandre relied on their tenacity, although he knew that his employees took advantage of the night to whisper among themselves and to agree on ways to rebel, first against France, then later against him, and through him against the United States. During the day, he had to negotiate with the American army the number of trees to cut down to allow the trucks, jeeps, and tanks to pass through, in exchange for protection against bombs and the spraying of defoliants.

The coolies knew that the rubber trees were worth more than their lives. And so, they hid under the broad canopy formed by trees still unharmed, whether they were employees, rebels, or both. Alexandre's distress at the prospect of waking one night to the spectacle of his plantation on fire was concealed beneath his unbleached linen suit. He suppressed his fear of being killed in his sleep by surrounding himself with servants and young women, his *con gái*.

On days when rubber shares hit a new low or the trucks transporting bales of rubber were ambushed on their way to port, Alexandre roamed through the rows of trees seeking a hand with delicate fingers that might unclench his fist, a compliant tongue that could unblock his gritted teeth, a narrow passage between two legs that would contain his rage.

While they may have been illiterate and couldn't dream of travelling beyond Vietnam's borders, the coolies understood that elsewhere in the world synthetic rubber was making inroads. They experienced the same fears as Alexandre, which spurred a number of them to leave the plantation and forge new paths in the cities, in the large centres where the American presence—soon in the tens of thousands—created new possibilities, new ways of living and dying. Some reinvented themselves as sellers of Spam, sunglasses, or grenades. Those who were able to quickly master the musicality of the English language would become interpreters. As for the most daring, they chose to vanish into tunnels dug beneath the feet of the American soldiers. They died as double agents, between two lines of fire or under four metres of earth, torn apart by bombs or eaten away by the larvae that embedded themselves beneath the skin.

The day when Alexandre realized that the application of Agent Orange on the neighbouring forests had poisoned a quarter of his plantation's trees and that his foreman had had his throat cut in his sleep by a Communist resistance commando, he screamed.

He took out his feelings on Mai, who happened to be in his path, somewhere between fury and despair.

Mai

At the time of colonization, France had regarded Indochina, and Vietnam along with it, as a zone of economic operation rather than as a colony to be settled. The French were able to enter the race for rubber by planting trees. It took a lot of determination to keep groups of agricultural workers in one place, in the middle of the bush, to uproot bamboo forests whose roots were thickly tangled in the soil, then to embed the rubber trees before harvesting their sap from one dawn to the next. Every drop of latex obtained was worth the drop of blood or sweat it had cost. The rubber trees could be bled for twenty-five or thirty years, while one man in four among the eighty thousand coolies sent into the plantations succumbed long before. Those thousands of dead, amid the whispering leaves, the murmuring branches, and the breath of the wind, still seek the reason why, during their lifetime, they replaced their tropical forest with trees from the Amazon, why they mutilated them, why they blindly obeyed those tall men with such pale cheeks and such hairy skin who in no way resembled their own elders, with their bony bodies and their ebony hair.

Mai had the copper skin of the coolies, and Alexandre the posture of an owner who was a monarch in his domain. Alexandre came to Mai in anger. Mai came to Alexandre in hate.

COOLIE

This word had been in use in many countries, on five continents, since the previous century. It referred first and foremost to workers from China and India, transported on the same boats and by the same captains as in the time of slavery.

Upon arrival at their destination, the coolies worked as hard as beasts on sugar cane plantations, down in mines, building railroads, often dying before the end of their five-year contract without having received their promised and longed-for salary. Companies involved in the trade assumed beforehand that twenty, thirty, or forty percent of the "lots" would perish in the course of the voyage at sea. The Indians and the Chinese who outlived their contracts in the British, French, or Dutch colonies settled in the Seychelles; in Trinidad and Tobago; in the Fiji Islands; Barbados; Guadeloupe; Martinique; in Canada, the United States . . . Before the Cuban Revolution, the largest Chinatown in Latin America was in Havana.

Unlike the Indian coolies, who included in their ranks women fleeing abusive husbands or desperate situations, the Chinese coolies were exclusively male—Chinese women didn't take the bait. The Chinese exiled in distant colonies with no possibility of returning home sought consolation in the arms of local women. All those who did not succumb to suicide, malnutrition, or abuse organized themselves to publish newspapers, create clubs, and open restaurants. Thanks to the dispersal of those men, fried rice, soy sauce, and wonton soup became favourites all over the planet.

As for the Indian coolie men, they had one chance in three of wooing an Indian woman, as many of them also embarked on an adventure that would transform the status of women and the distinction between castes. They were in a position to choose, even to receive a dowry rather than provide one. This new power engendered a fear in men of not having a woman or of losing one. Neighbours, passersby, and the women themselves were a threat to them. Some men shut their wives up in strongbox houses, others wound ropes around them like ribbons on a gift box. When men's fears are confronted by women's power, the result is deadly.

The Chinese and Indian slaves and coolies were wrenched away from their native lands, while the

Vietnamese coolies stayed at home and laboured under comparable conditions imposed by expatriate settlers.

Alexandre and Mai

14 Mai had been assigned to infiltrate Alexandre's plantation. She was happy to be able to save a few trees every day, making an incision that was too deep, thereby preventing the sap from running again, stopping the flow to the detriment of the boss's profit. She rose every morning at four o'clock to assert her love of country by destroying her boss Alexandre, inflicting on his property a long, slow death, one tree at a time, one incision at a time, like the death by a thousand cuts of Chinese emperors.

Her love for Alexandre put an end to her mission.

Alexandre had dragged Mai by her hair all the way to his room. He had ordered her to perform the usual services of his *con gái*. Not only had Mai refused, but she had thrown herself at him, hatchet in hand, ready to slice his throat at a forty-five-degree angle.

Mai intended to kill Alexandre or, at the very least, to chase him from the property, then from the country. Alexandre was an old wolf, hardened by the wealth of latex, by the stings of fire ants, and by the hot winds that burned his Gallic skin.

She had been waiting for this moment ever since she'd arrived at the plantation. Driven by the desire to kill, to avenge her people, she had rushed at Alexandre's eyes, two jade balls. Mai was unsettled by the serenity of his gaze, her incendiary momentum instantly stopped short by the sudden feeling that she had gone back to her native village, to the dense green calm of Ha Long Bay. As for Alexandre, in his profound weariness from being loved by no one, he'd given up, hoping for a long rest, the end of a hundred-year-long struggle perpetuating itself in this foreign land that by force of circumstance had become his own.

If researchers had got wind of the love story between Mai and Alexandre, maybe the Stockholm Syndrome would have been called the Tây Ninh Syndrome, or Bên Cui, or Xa Cam. Mai, a steadfast teenager, possessed by the mission she'd been assigned to, had not known to be wary of love and its absurdities. She didn't know that the impulses of the heart can be more blinding than the noonday sun, with no warning or logic. Love, like death, need not knock twice in order to be heard.

This lightning strike that became love between Mai and Alexandre would ultimately sow discord in their circles. The idealistic and romantic dreamers wanted to see in it the possibility of a better world, symbiotic, entangled. The realists and the politically committed would condemn the recklessness, the carelessness of blurring limits while reversing roles.

On this landscape of closeness and rivalry, the birth of Tâm, child of the master and his labourer, two enemies, still had something about it that was ordinary and banal.

Tâm, Alexandre, and Mai

In the tender, protective cocoon provided by her little family, Tâm grew up between Alexandre's privilege and power, and the shame of Mai's betrayal of her patriotic cause. The birthday cakes iced with buttercream traced a tangible border between her and the children in the village where the coolies and their families lived. Alexandre and Mai, her parents, the nanny, the gardener, and the cooks formed an enclosure so narrow that she never had a chance to play with the workers' children. But on the day when the warring camps decided to fight openly, all found themselves together on the same battlefield. Bullets make no distinction between the man who dries rubber with smoke and the girl who takes piano lessons. He who hauls a hundred-kilogram roll of compressed latex and he who uses his hands only for lovemaking receive the same treatment before breathing their last. Before the appearance of drones, before ranged attacks, before it was possible to kill without sullying either eyes or hands, combat zones were likely the only places where human beings became equal to each other through their mutual annihilation.

So it was that the fates of Alexandre and Mai were bound up forever with those of the workers, all fallen in the same place, the bodies of some piled onto others under the debris and in silence and horror, amid showers of sparks sifting through rows of trees.

Taking refuge between the impregnable strongbox—now turned into a shield—and a sideboard full of dishes, the nanny was able to protect Tâm, and became her de facto mother.

Tâm and the Nanny

The nanny took Tâm from their hiding place during the first lull, when the only noise, repetitive, tearing through the villa bathed in light, was that of the fan blades. They ran together in the opposite direction from the factory, their breath matching the rhythm of their steps, the birds silenced, far from the bodies being drained of their identities, of their senses. Naked, the earth was no longer a dance floor for sun and leaves. The tropical climate was now brutal, unfiltered, pitiless. Thanks to the generosity of a boy leading his buffalo, a soldier driving his jeep, a potter transporting empty jars, they arrived at the nanny's native village a few weeks later. Her face coated in dust, Tâm was introduced to her new "big brother" and her new "grandmother." The filth of the road had darkened her fair hair and her caramel eyes, the winds had dulled her dress's red roses. Like a cut flower, her childhood faded before it had bloomed.

Tâm lived at My Lai for three years. From the

"grandmother," she learned how to glean the grains of rice that fell from the bundles of straw during beating and winnowing. In My Lai and other villages, many children were raised by their grandparents. Out of necessity, the family members supported the person most likely to obtain the best-paying job. Out of duty, whoever secured the job in return saw to their needs. Out of love, parents, fathers or mothers, left their children behind so they wouldn't have to watch them consoling themselves after the shower of insults received in the pigsty or the house, while gathering up the shards of shattered bowls thrown down on their heads.

The Servant Girl and Alexandre

Alexandre's servant had waited more than two decades before rising to the position of nanny when Tâm was born. She was the only one to have survived the storms, outside and inside, the boundless despondencies, the senseless excesses of her employer. She could read the worries in the sound of his heels on the tiles. She alone sensed the burden of his homesickness and his resistance to putting down roots in Vietnam. In the beginning, he had worn his jacket and behaved as an engineer in front of his predecessors with their shirts half-open, wrinkled, and soiled. He forced himself to sit up straight in his chair to avoid developing the loose tongue of his compatriots. Unlike the older owners, he plunged his hands into the red earth to feel it at the same time as the natives. But slowly, perniciously, his body began to resemble that of his counterparts. Unconsciously, he had little by little let his hand come down on the backs of his coolies' necks, blaming them for a drop in production instead of inspecting the poisoned roots of his trees. He became an old warrior worn down by monsoons, by financial uncertainties and disillusionment, resembling the other owners more and more.

At the age of fifteen, a single mother separated from her child, the servant girl became his employee. She started as the maid of the maid of the head maid. She was the last to eat the remains of meals—even if it was she who had plucked the chicken, scaled the fish, and minced the pork. On the day her immediate superior left, she inherited the cleaning to be done in Alexandre's bedroom: in other words, it was up to her to see to her employer's well-being without attracting notice. Studying the folds in his sheets, she could tell on what nights his worries had frozen Alexandre on the edge of his bed, head between his hands. Noting the presence of ebony hairs and the places where they were found, she could almost describe the choreography of his lovemaking. The years spent in Alexandre's wake taught her his logic when it came to hiding some of his savings. She became the guardian of a great book emptied of its pages and packed with bundles of bills and gold rings strung on a chain that was also twenty-four carat gold. She checked the stiff cover every day to erase the marks of Alexandre's fingers. This would make it hard for thieves to distinguish the volume from the others on the shelf. She was the shadow that followed Alexandre's shadow. His guardian angel.

The Nanny and Tâm

24 Tâm's arrival allowed the servant to take on the more maternal role of nanny, to rediscover the smiles she'd missed after leaving behind her own son with her mother in My Lai. Now the employees called her *Chị Vú*, or "big sister breast." Rich women sometimes hired a young mother to breastfeed their child, so as not to deform their own breasts. The Vietnamese language is very modest, but the word *breast* is uttered with no hesitation or embarrassment, as breasts suggest no eroticism in this context. Since female employers rented the breasts of *Chị Vú* women, they were able to treat them as objects, demanding that they nurse the employer's child exclusively. Some *Chị Vú* tried to run to their own offspring at nightfall, risking retaliation and dismissal. Most became attached to the infant they fed, because their own, to whom they'd given birth, lived fifty, or a hundred, or five hundred kilometres away. Employers relinquished their maternal privilege in the name of beauty, never suspecting

that their children would become more attached to the scent of their *Chị Vú* than to that of the imported eau de toilette they sprayed on their skin.

The nanny did not breastfeed Tâm. She raised her, running after her with a spoon, transforming mealtimes into a game of hide-and-seek between two friends.

Tâm and the Lycée

In My Lai, Tâm's nanny carried her on her bicycle, pedalling for kilometres to take her to piano lessons. She mended her pants dozens of times, rather than open the book full of rings and money that she'd made off with when they fled. During the day, she encouraged Tâm to take a seat on her school bench; at night, she protected her from curious gazes by having her lie down between herself and the grandmother.

To respect the wishes of Alexandre and Mai, she sought help from the region's teachers to fill out the forms that would allow Tâm to take the admission exam for Saigon's most prestigious school. The Gia Long Lycée had survived resettlements, occupations, and changes to its mission while still preserving its reputation. At the time it was founded at the beginning of the twentieth century, when it was called the College for Young Native Girls, the French language was compulsory, except during the two hours per week when Vietnamese literature was taught.

A few decades later, teaching in the Vietnamese language was included in the courses, soon followed by English. Each year, only ten percent of the thousands of girls who arrived from all over to take the exam were admitted. The competition attracted the best because the graduates could marry well and, coincidentally, become activists or even revolutionaries.

The nanny was of the opinion that Tâm should leave My Lai for the city of Saigon, which would offer every opportunity, unlike the village that obliged her to be submissive, to hunch her shoulders in order to deflect the ugly words of gossips.

The day before their long bus trip, the nanny stayed awake all night to chase away mosquitoes and keep Tâm cool, gently waving a fan over her back; when the girl woke, a *bánh mì* with pork sausage, cucumber, and fresh coriander was waiting. She had also prepared sticky rice balls with fresh peanuts, wrapped in banana leaves. Then she had made packages of dried cuttlefish to give to the Saigon innkeeper, a former plantation worker.

The street in front of the lycée was teeming with mothers, aunties, women. During the two-day exam, the nanny obsessively rolled her rosary beads between her fingers. Needless to say, neither God nor Buddha could answer the prayers of all the people on the sidewalk, as they were hundreds of times more numerous than the available places. The nurse pleaded then with the soul of Mai, who ought to know the answers to the exam, since she had already passed this test.

When Tâm's name appeared on the list of students admitted to the lycée, the nurse knew that Mai's spirit had been watching over her daughter.

FRANCE

France rooted itself in Vietnam by cultivating its land. The country entrenched itself so thoroughly that the Vietnamese still use at least a hundred French words every day without being aware of it.

café: *cà phê* (coffee)
gâteau: *ga-tô* (cake)
beurre: *bơ* (butter)
pâté: *pa-tê*
antenne: ăng-ten (antenna)
parabole: *parabôn* (parabola)
gant: *găng* (glove)
crème: *kem/cà rem* (cream)
bille: *bi* (marble)
bière: *bia* (beer)
moteur: *mô tơ* (motor)
chemise: *sơ mi* (shirt)
dentelle: *đăng ten* (lace)

poupée: *búp bê* (doll)
moto: *mô tô* (motorbike)
compas: *com pa* (compass)
équipe: *ê kíp* (team)
Noël: *nô en* (Christmas)
scandale: *xì căng đan* (scandal)
guitare: *ghi ta* (guitar)

radio: *ra dô*
taxi: *tắc xi*
galant: *ga lăng* (courteous)
chef: *sếp*

Each of these words is part of everyday Vietnamese life. In exchange, French settlers acquired some Vietnamese words. They pronounced them according to the habits of their own language, sometimes expanding them, giving them a second meaning. *Con gái* didn't just mean "girl," but also "prostitute." Prostitute above all. Only prostitute.

Alexandre never uttered the word *con gái* again after Tâm's birth, even though she was a girl. Because she was his daughter.

The Nanny and Tâm in Saigon

The nurse honoured the love between Mai and Alexandre by moving to Saigon to take care of Tâm as a mother would, in the role of her mother. Every day, she was waiting for Tâm after her classes with a glass of green herbal juice filled with ice cubes. Others copied her, believing that the vitamins in *rau má* were the reason for the girl's excellent grades. The nanny preferred this drink to sugar cane juice because of the word *má*, which means "mama." She wanted Tâm to hear the word *má* spoken every day. This routine was observed without fail during the first year of her studies at the lycée. The gold rings were sold off as needed—paying for everything from the rental of a former shed, two metres by five, squeezed between two new buildings, to a bottle of mauve ink, to underwear, and right down to four barrettes to hold back her fine hair during classes.

The nanny had sewn the remaining rings into two pockets doubly hidden in her white cotton blouse, which she wore under another long-sleeved blouse whose wine-red colour had faded in the sun. Protected by her old conical hat, she glided through the streets among thieves, criminals, and the curious, like a shadow with no soul or history. Without her, the city's wolves would have made short work of Tâm. Even though she wore a white uniform identical to those of her friends, even though she wore her hair in two braids like most of the students her age, her luminous complexion dazzled the most jaded eyes. Fortunately, Tâm's strong shoulders discouraged people accustomed to the traditional idea of beauty that extolled discretion in a woman. From one age to another, poets celebrated the grace of sloping shoulders. From one era to another, designers of the Vietnamese tunic were determined to provide it with raglan sleeves that held in place the two pieces of cloth with a seam going from the collar to the armpit, thereby avoiding any emphasis on the physique. It was hard for foreigners to imagine the strength of those shoulders that bore the heavy yokes transporting both soups and bricks for sale, not to mention glass and the metal from exploded shells to recycle.

No one could have suspected that Tâm's nanny was capable of carrying five dozen cobs of corn in one basket and a charcoal oven in the other. She offered passersby choices for their corn: boiled or grilled, seasoned with green onion sauce. She roamed the neighbourhood during class hours, but never later. If she wasn't able to sell everything, she gave what was left over to the neighbourhood beggars.

The Nanny and Tâm at My Lai

During a school holiday, the nanny decided to go back to My Lai to celebrate the arrival of the first baby born to her son and his new bride. Tâm chose to bring as a present two sets of T-shirts and matching shorts, and the nanny, a jar of talc, a baby bottle, a hat, and a small gold chain with a thin pendant. On their arrival, the nanny, along with the neighbours, prepared a feast worthy of a king to celebrate her grandchild's first month, an event that marks the end of a critical period for the newborn, and his entry into a new life. The nanny went to sleep, amid the scent of the baby's skin, which she had been inhaling happily all day. Tâm, as usual, lay at her side on the mat of the bamboo bed.

Usually, the nanny woke at dawn. The day after the celebration, weariness kept her in bed until helicopters appeared above the rice paddies, like a swarm of insects. The peasants did not fear the soldiers because of their grenades and machine guns; rather, they dreaded their unpredictability. But since the village was accustomed to surprise patrols, the neighbours went on with their breakfast, the nanny's childhood friend left for the market, the sage recited a poem from his hammock, and the children ran towards the soldiers arriving on foot, hoping to be given chocolates, pencils, and candies. No one suspected that they were going to set fire to the huts while shooting their weapons with the same eagerness at chickens and humans.

The night before, Tâm had lain down a child; the next day, she awoke with no family. She went from artless laughter to the silence of adults whose tongues have been cut out. In four hours, her long, girlish braids were undone, as she faced the spectre of scalped heads.

Take Care of Them

36 Had she been asked, the nanny would have chosen to die at the same time as the sow and in place of her neighbour so as not to have witnessed the rape of her girls. As she was begging the aggressors not to bash through the door of Tâm's body and that of her daughter-in-law, nor to slash them with their knives, as their brothers in arms were doing, she saw out of the corner of her eye a soldier in the process of hiding behind a pile of straw and firing a bullet into his foot. His comrades thought he was screaming because of his wound, but she knew that he was screaming before, long before, his head buried between his thighs. She had four hours to see the villagers burned alive in their underground hiding place, have their ears cut off, their chests shot through. She saw people terrorized, devastated, incredulous, and also defiant.

She was there when a soldier received the order to push a small group towards the irrigation canal surrounding the rice fields. The soldier thought he was being ordered to keep them under his watch: "*Take care of them.*" Since the time is passing slowly in the company of these unarmed people, the soldier starts talking to the children, humming a nursery rhyme, miming "Jack and Jill went up the hill," making big bubbles with his chewing gum. He's relieved to have been given this task, because the fear of having to open up the underground hiding places had made him piss himself. He never knew how many people might be waiting in these holes of different depths. One metre, two metres, five metres? With or without grenades? With or without bamboo spears, their tips coated in urine and feces, waiting to pierce his body? At the age of nineteen, his memory is still fresh of the games of hide-and-seek with his siblings and cousins. He was one of those children who was as startled to discover his friends in hiding as when he was caught himself. His father would have been proud to see him looking down on his enemies crouched on their heels even though he had not yet experienced his first love. Fortunately, his father would never see the image of the soldier weeping in front of his superior who'd come to shout in his face: "*Take care of them!*" That was when he'd closed his eyes and emptied the magazine of his machine gun.

Some months later, the politicians and judges would show him the photo of a nearly naked baby, lying askew and face down on the pile of corpses, like the cherry on a sundae.

"I was ordered to kill everything that moved."

"Civilians?"

"Yes."

"Old people?"

"Yes."

"Women?"

"Yes, women."

"Babies?"

"Babies."

The answers would come naturally to him, without his having to think. He wasn't the only one who could stay stony-hearted. There was the soldier who would comment on the photo where the nanny has her shoulders square and her back tense. He maintained that he spared the nanny, her son, her grandson, and her daughter-in-law from suffering, by eliminating them. The photographer probably received the order to capture the moment as it was happening, with a view to future studies on human behaviour. Thirty seconds from a death that is unannounced but certain, each person reacts differently. That day, there were a number of options: being burned alive, buried alive, or felled by a bullet.

Standing between a hundred-year-old tree and

the photographer's lens, the nanny looks terrified, as if already she sees death advancing towards them. Her son embraces his mother with his entire body, and his young wife clutches their child while she fastens the last button on her blouse. In the photo, you can see the triangle of skin just above her navel; her face is abnormally calm, eyes down, her gaze intense; her hair is newly tied up; her clothes are wrinkled and covered in dust. Long after, the photographer would wonder if the click of his shutter hadn't triggered the firing of the soldier's machine gun. In a slow, measured tone, he would attest that the young woman had been raped and that she was in the process of putting her clothes back on when she fell beneath the bullets. Her fingers were trying in vain to press down on the snap fastener while her baby's legs were pulling aside her blouse.

She fell before she'd had time to raise her head and look into the lens.

Tâm without the Nanny

Tâm had been pushed into the ravine. She did not witness her nanny's final moments, just as she had not seen her parents die. And so she could believe that they were entwined in the garden hammock, near the bougainvillea hedge, and that they never emerged from their deep lovers' sleep to greet death.

Tâm imagined that her nanny had managed to escape and was now living with her grandson in a remote village in the mountains. In the ravine, Tâm had thought she had been hit by the gunshots of the soldier who had finally understood his superior's order. In fact, she fainted when the head of a baby, bound to his mother's chest by a strip of cloth, burst into fragments before her eyes.

POINTS OF VIEW

The Americans speak of the "Vietnam War," the Vietnamese of the "American War." This distinction is perhaps what explains the cause of that war. 41

Tâm and the Pilot in My Lai

42 If Tâm had known that a helicopter pilot was to spot her as she was disentangling herself from the pile of inert bodies, she would not have moved. Unlike the baby who had been killed by a second gunshot because he had screamed, Tâm didn't need a mother's breast in her mouth to make her stay silent and play dead. The blood of others was running into her ear, making it seem to her that she was being protected by hell, that realm forbidden to humans. But death is not given to us all.

The pilot saw Tâm's hair rippling down her back, just like the hair of his daughter Diane, whom he'd put to bed a few months, a few days, a few hours earlier.

The pilot saw life. The aircraft descended towards Tâm, and he pulled her away from the corpses washed in light. The man lifted her, tugging on her sodden blouse, stained with indelible images. He climbed, holding her at the end of his arm, straight up towards the sky.

The pilot gave life a chance. Gave himself a chance at

his own life, the one that awaited him after the war, after My Lai, after Tâm, when he would rejoin his own people.

The Soldier (or the War Machine)

44 When the soldier who killed the nanny and her family resumed civilian life, he recounted with detached enthusiasm how he'd survived the trap of the three-step snakes, whose venom killed in a flash, and that of the exploding grenade tied onto the enemy flag he'd wanted to make away with as a souvenir when his battalion had taken the village. He had the arrogance of someone who, during his deployment, passed a few centimetres from death; who a few seconds earlier or later might have been blown to smithereens, and who was always just a breath away from his last expiration. He got married and brought up his child with confidence and abandon until the day his son received a stray bullet in the head while running behind his dog. From then on, the former soldier sat motionless in his armchair fourteen hours a day, his whole body trembling despite the medications he was on. He dared not sleep because the picture of the woman's body that he had turned onto her back was imprinted behind his

eyelids. When he closed his eyes, he saw again his panic when confronted with the exploded head of the baby still glued to its mother's chest. He had no memory of later victims. He had shouldered his M16, then fired with open eyes in order to drown his first two victims in a sea of the newly dead. He had buried them all and had drowned himself in alcohol until the day of his son's funeral.

When the framed photo of the boy fell to the ground, the shattered glass took him back to the dike where he became a robot; where the machine mounted in his head kicked into gear; and where a single word began to turn in a loop: *kill.* He refused to let his wife buy a new frame. From the moment he settled in the armchair beside the damaged photograph, he began to poison himself, swallowing twenty pills a day, hoping finally to go and recover his son and to kneel down before that woman and her baby, alive. Time would recede, become virgin again, and would begin anew at the origin of the world.

Tâm could describe in detail how the soldiers slipped the ace of spades into their helmet straps, sleeves rolled up above their elbows, the cuffs of their pant legs tucked into their boots. On the other hand, she remembered no soldier's face. Maybe war machines don't have a human face.

Tâm, the Pilot, and the Sky

46 In her memory, only one soldier seemed human. He had round cheeks and soft skin. When the American pilot pulled her up by her blouse, she had the sky behind her. This invisible hand wrenched her at lightning speed away from the bloodbath, her compatriots, her history. During the flight, she understood that not only was she alive, but she was going to touch heaven thanks to this soldier with cheeks as rosy as those of Alexandre, her father.

Tâm and the Sisters

She was never able to say just when she'd been brought down to earth and entrusted to the nursing sisters, those women faithful to their God and devoted to those who were uprooted.

For three years, Tâm grew up sheltered in their arms, in communion with the easy laughter of orphans who had everything to gain.

Tâm and Madame Naomi

On January 11, 1973, the sisters asked Tâm to accompany a child to Saigon and deliver him to his adoptive parents. This trip, which was to last only forty-eight hours, was extended because of late flights, winter storms, and new military strategies. Tâm slept curled up with the child on the floor of the Saigon orphanage founded by Madame Naomi. New babies arrived there every day through the front door, through the side window, through the neighbouring alleyway, often after dark, but also in the middle of the day, when the women's vision was blurred by perspiration. Her stay dragged on for another week. Without a sigh or a blink, Tâm set to work, plunging her hands at once into the big pail of soapy water filled with tiny shorts and square cloths that served as diapers when folded into triangles. She shook dust off the mats and swept the floor the way her nanny did, going from the edge towards the centre.

Since Tâm had studied at the lycée, the density and

frantic activity in the city were familiar to her. That is why Madame Naomi gave her the task of picking up from a hotel a box of powdered milk offered by American donors. Tâm didn't know that she was about to cross the threshold of the General Headquarters of the CIA, and that, in the entrance hall, men in ties were trying to silence the pilot with rosy cheeks.

The Pilot and His Homeland

Three years earlier, when the pilot had decided to reach out the open door to pull the teenaged girl out of the ravine, he was prepared to open fire on his brothers in arms, or to be shot down by them. The military family and then, in his country, his compatriots, his political leaders, reproached him for having lined up his personal values in opposition to loyalty to his motherland. His action poured some good into evil and muddled strength and innocence. His indictment, the arguments and debates that followed, threw him into a dark and clamorous vortex, with no escape.

It was only now, in the foyer of the hotel used by the CIA, that there came his moment of grace, at the sight of Tâm's modest grey dress, modelled on those of the sisters in the orphanage, minus the embroidered collar.

The Pilot and Tâm in Saigon

The pilot and Tâm did not recognize each other. But their eyes met. His attraction to her was so strong that he dared to walk away from his discussion with the men in ties in order to join her. He went to see her at the orphanage that night, and the next day, and the next.

He persuaded her to stay in Saigon, to wait for him in Saigon, to love him in Saigon. He set her up in an apartment in the heart of the city, near the Bến Thành central market, near the presidential palace, near the hotels, far from the battlefields, far from him. The pilot and the young girl knew three days and three nights of love.

The first night, the pilot untied Tâm's hair and caressed her left ear. He saw the missing lobe, which resembled the one, half torn off, that had dropped into his hand as he leaned the girl back on the side of the helicopter. He spent the night asking forgiveness, and she, loving him. When his gaze fell into hers, the conflict within him, between the man and the soldier, disappeared. He finally admitted that he'd been right to defy human folly and to manage to preserve what was left of innocence. On the third day, the pilot had to return to his base. He would come back. Tâm waited for him for three hours, three days, three years. She went on waiting for him but no longer counted the weeks, the months, the decades. Because those three days with him had been eternities, her eternities.

Tâm was soon taken on by one of the thousand nightclubs that had sprung up like mushrooms in the city. Outside her apartment, the clink of key rings between fingers moving off down the hallway, the silence of air currents in the corridor, and the repeated threats of eviction all forced her to consent to nourishing the starving with her flesh. She hoped to hear again the timbre of the pilot's voice among the soldiers demanding from her acts of love. Every coupling stabbed her heart. She clung to life and kept waiting for him even as the pilot's death had already been communicated to his wife and daughter, somewhere on the other side of the Pacific, in San Diego. No one told her that the pilot had been accidentally crushed by the wheel of a plane. The weight of the aircraft had flattened his heart, too dazed from love to take basic precautions. He died just as he was recovering, for the first time since My Lai, the desire to breathe deeply into his lungs.

Tâm and the Soldiers in Saigon

His fellow soldiers said among themselves that the pilot's death had happened so quickly that it didn't have time to erase his smile.

Tâm remained completely unaware. In her solitude, she received propositions from soldiers with wounds that were invisible but detectable to the touch in the half-light, like phosphorescent algae in the ocean waves that are only visible after nightfall. The fear and anguish of these men soothed her own feelings, the weight of their tense bodies relieved the weight on hers. Some fell in love with Tâm, with her English sprinkled with French words and spiced with a Vietnamese accent. Pressed against her, they dreamed of the ordinary, of an unremarkable life with her in Austin, Cedar Rapids, Trenton . . . She always gave her blessing to their dreams, pressing her hand on their cheek before letting them go back to a jungle packed tight with giant elephant leaves, with grasses that sliced like razor blades in forests overrun with flying-tiger traps that pounced on them with iron teeth and claws of steel.

R & R

56 The army granted soldiers five days of leave after their third month of service. The soldiers could choose from a long list of destinations in order of preference. Lovers often chose Hawaii—to reunite with their American girlfriends on American soil. Electronics and camera fanatics flew off to Japan and Taiwan, while Hong Kong and Singapore attracted those who wanted to enhance their wardrobe before heading home. Australia was popular because there they could find women who saw them as heroes, who spoke their own language, and had familiar faces.

They could also choose to stay in Vietnam, visit the Vung Tau beaches, or plunge into the prodigious whirlwind of Saigon. Wherever they landed, a team was waiting to warn them of the traps that awaited them in the bars. Because their superiors knew in advance that most of the soldiers would spend their leave in the experienced arms of women who knew better than they did themselves their fantasies, their demons, and their wants. But since time was short, the only possible comfort they could offer was alcohol and counterfeit acts of love, like the ones in movies. The soldiers returned to the jungle fulfilled; the women had faithfully attended to their needs. As time went on, the idea of the R & R, an abbreviation for *rest and recreation*, was clarified as *rape and run* or *rape and ruin.* Other shorthand just as realistic was added, such as A & A for *ass and alcohol*, I & I for *intercourse and intoxication*, and P & P for *pussy and popcorn.*

When the soldiers returned to base, the army provided medication to treat those who showed signs of unwanted souvenirs between their legs. But it did not plan any intercession to eliminate the seeds they'd sown inside the bodies of some of the women. That is why Asian populations that were once homogeneous, such as that of South Vietnam, became diversified, with children who had hair pale or curly, eyes round and long-lashed, skin dark or freckled, almost always fatherless and also, often, without a mother.

Louis

58 Another little boy born with no name. The manioc seller, with her orange, blue, and white sweet potatoes, gave him a sheet of transparent plastic to protect him from the rain. She called him *mỹ đen*, or "Black American." The barber who hung his mirror on the rusted nail on a tree every morning for decades preferred to call him *con lai*, "half-breed child," and sometimes simply *đen*. The woman who every night had to add twigs to her broom to clean the sidewalk breastfed Louis at the same time as her own baby, whose complexion was almost the same. This nursing mother did not give him a name, because she was born mute; or perhaps she became so after having played dead in order to survive a routine visit to her village; or perhaps she lost her power of speech when her son was born, the colour of his body the same as the charred bodies of her mother and cousins. No one knew, because no one asked. That's how it was in this corner of the world, at this corner of the sidewalk.

One afternoon, on this same sidewalk, a young woman coming out of a bar left the door ajar long enough for a lingering goodbye kiss with her American soldier, who could have been, at nineteen or twenty, with his first lover. The music from inside flooded the space all the way into the street, where the local rickshaw driver was parked. The driver didn't know all the soldiers who spent time in this bar, but he could predict the consequences of every languorous embrace. He had many times ferried these young girls to those older women who knew how to do away with the traces of those short-lived romances. Sometimes it was the young girls themselves who had to abandon the dance floor and the bar long enough to bring a child into the world.

Louis was not the first baby to turn up at the foot of the tamarinds, like a ripe fruit fallen from the tree or a seedling pushing up from the earth. No one was surprised, then. Some took care of him, giving him a cardboard box, rice water, clothing. In the street, the older children adopted the younger ones as the days passed, creating fleeting families.

You had to wait until the child's personality asserted itself before choosing a name. Sometimes the children were identified by a nickname: *con què* ("crippled leg girl") or *thằng thẹo* ("scar boy"). In the case of Louis, it was thanks to Louis Armstrong's voice that often escaped from the half-open bar door after the noon siesta.

The rickshaw driver was happy to have had this bright idea, to have made the connection between Armstrong's dark skin and Louis's. Perhaps in that way he wanted to encourage Louis to imagine the softness of the *clouds of white* despite the heat of the concrete under his behind, to smell the perfume of *red roses* and not the odour of his own urine, to see *the colours of the rainbow* when the mosquitoes sang too loudly around his head, when he was chased away by the broom along with the trash, when he salivated in front of people noisily slurping their boiling hot noodles to cool them off just a little, just enough. All to the rhythm of the music of this *wonderful world.*

Louis's Mothers

By the age of six or seven, Louis had already mastered the art of thrusting a long hook through the wrought iron grilles on windows to pull out a fried fish, a ring, a wallet. When his hands brushed the pockets of passersby, bills flew out as fast as a wingbeat. From the beginning, he could identify in the blink of an eye someone's *tim đen*, the seat of desire and weakness.

The mother who had nursed him had wanted to keep him alive to rent him out to professional beggars. A soft-limbed baby conferred a nobly maternal air on the outstretched hand of a woman in rags. As well, the wild eyes, blank face, and dusty cheeks of a malnourished infant incited people to act as the righters of wrongs.

Louis could differentiate the perfumes of his mothers-for-a-day. The one who rummaged in the corner garbage heaps smelled of life brought to the boil and the sum of the neighbourhood residents' secrets. The lottery ticket seller gave off a smell of damp earth, while the water carrier exuded coolness. When Louis was old enough to walk, he accompanied a blind singer who, with the aid of a portable tape recorder, played dramatic excerpts from traditional musical comedies. Louis soon learned that the more the speaker crackled, the sooner the people dropped their money into his plastic bucket.

His mothers taught Louis how to roam the street's kiosks to gather up what was left in the bowls before their owners could chase him away. Some clients left, on purpose or absent-mindedly, a slice of meat at the bottom of their soup. Others, out of embarrassment, preferred to toss a bone and its marrow on the ground for a stray dog to pick up, rather than offer it to Louis. Some would drop a paper napkin into what was left of their soup, under the famished eyes of the beggars. Often, those clients found that their dishes did not arrive quickly enough or that their *phở* lacked cinnamon or smelled too strongly of star anise.

In the course of stalking and seeking out leftovers, Louis learned to read the customers' personalities. He guessed who warmed their taste buds with powerful chili pepper so that their tongues could spit words of fire at their unfaithful spouses. He could distinguish which drops of sweat on the side of a face were caused by hot broth, and which were incited by nervousness. Louis knew that drumming fingers were sending messages. In that case, it was better to distance oneself from those coded conversations, because in a conflict zone, innocence was no excuse once one had attained the age of reason. At the age of seven, you start to be able to tell good from evil, justice from a dream, deeds from intentions. At seven, you can show up at a terrace full of soldiers to clean their boots still spattered with blood, or to set off a grenade, depending on what the adults have commanded. At seven, you're supposed to have emerged from your Oedipal phase, a stage utterly removed from Louis's development. In any case, Louis's age varied depending on the patchy memories of the neighbourhood beggars.

Louis and Tâm

64 Beneath Tâm's balcony, cigarette sellers, stray dogs, and the child-adults, including Louis, wandered by. At the age of eight, when Tâm came to live in the neighbourhood, Louis was already an old hand, intimately familiar with the temperature of the asphalt under his feet in the daytime and under his back at night. In the shade of the flame trees, he made conversation with the drivers of the official cars who were waiting for their bosses while playing Chinese checkers, the generals' game. On the sidewalk, he showed visitors the way to the post office and the location of the go-go bars behind the signs advertising "restaurants." He spent his days roaming the streets with the legless beggar, lying face down at ground level on a skateboard. Louis cleared the way for him, dividing the crowd into three: the guilty hearts, the compassionate hearts, and the hardened hearts. He knew when to stand motionless, to wait for people to pull money out of their pockets, or for the moment when he could himself slip

in his hand. He was the nephew of one, the cousin of another, without a last name.

During the night, he regained his civil status, that of an orphan, more precisely a Black orphan who slept behind bushes or on benches in the square, who disappeared beneath the stars into the blackness of the open sky.

Louis and Pamela

66 When he became old enough to run after people with his box of rags and polish, offering to shine their shoes, Louis adopted an American woman who taught English in a training centre for the employees of Pan Am airline. Pamela liked to sit on a bench in the park and draw portraits of the children who hung out there, teaching them songs from her own childhood. What she saw in Louis and his street pals were models rich in texture, strong personalities, unsung geniuses. After a few rehearsals the group was singing the alphabet in unison.

Louis learned to write in the notebooks the young woman provided; he also traced letters in the dust. On very hot days, his sweat served as ink at the tips of his fingers on the granite of park benches.

The little ones clustered around Pamela, their childish laughter mingling with the words on the street, the same ones that people tossed off left and right, in no particular direction, in tune with angry outbursts and descents into hell. Pamela repeated after them these foreign sounds, rounding off the acute accents, softening the low notes, and lightening those that were weighty, because her English language could not modulate variations in tone as sharp as those in the Vietnamese language. Between them, a new language full of pleonasms was created. *OK được! Go đi! Má Pamela. Má* being Mama. The youngest preferred to call her *Má*mela.

Pamela told the children more than once that she had to leave to pursue her studies in Salt Lake City. Her children listened, and even consoled her. They said that it was normal that she would want to return to a city where you eat salt instead of fish sauce, that it was normal that she should leave them, because nothing was permanent.

Louis and Em Hồng

68 The day after Pamela left, a baby was abandoned under a park bench next to a sleeping Louis. At dawn, when one of his mothers wakened him with some swift kicks from a callused foot so that he'd go and deliver some coffees, he saw the baby. When he returned from his morning round, he realized that the baby had not moved. Improvising, he stole an empty instant noodle carton and placed inside it the little person with fair hair and closed eyes. Louis had a habit of assuming the role of Robin Hood within his ephemeral family, probably because of his tall stature and the cape Pamela had placed on his shoulders, to help explain the word *superhero*. People who own only the clothes on their backs know that they have to help each other out. Those who slit open the bottom of a purse to grab a wallet can count on the performance of their "blood brothers" joyously dancing around the victim. She who is exchanging a client's currency for Vietnamese *đồngs* counts the same bill twice because she knows that

other hands are there to tug at the customer's pants and shirt. That is why the new mother, the one who sold contraband Salems, Lucky Strikes, and Winstons, agreed to breastfeed the baby Louis found.

In time, Louis would feed the little girl himself with the dregs of bouillon and condensed milk right from the can he brought back from the market, weaving between cars and scooters. Now and then, he got from the woman who sold used boxes a brand new box that served as house, bedroom, and bed. Once, he stole a purple-and-yellow rattle from a child whose distracted mother was absorbed by a pair of gold lamé shoes displayed in a window.

Louis carried his baby on his back, using a strip of cloth, the way the other members of his ephemeral family carried their brother or sister. At night, he closed the top of the box to protect her from rats greedy for little toes. He was proud to be the one who gave her the name Hồng, a tribute to her cheeks, which were a soft pink despite the dust. The contrasting skin colours caught the eyes of passersby but did not surprise his clan, who were accustomed to the unlikely families being formed at random, according to circumstances and feelings. One adopts another while grasping a hand reaching up after a fall. One becomes an aunt, niece, or cousin while sharing a source of water, the corner of a lane, the base of a wall.

For months, Louis lived skin to skin with em Hồng, until the day when, on her way to the orphanage, Naomi heard the baby crying.

NAOMI

With one hand, she set up homes in Saigon to welcome orphans. With the other, she found people who wanted to be the parents of these children. In the course of her life, she gave birth five times, and carried more than seven hundred children.

She died alone. An orphan.

Naomi and Hồng

72 Naomi lifted Hồng out of her carton. Louis was sleeping beside her, his arms and legs surrounding the box. Naomi wanted to take them both to the orphanage, but Louis ran away. Instinctively, he ran into the night, like a thief. Ran for a long time. Wept for even longer. But, inevitably, dawn returned the next day, then the day after that, and every day following, without em Hồng.

The Bonze

The demonstrations multiplied, gatherings that were very lucrative for Louis and his friends. Their hands sauntered through the protesters' pockets, and their feet became lost in the crowd without leaving any traces. The streets, subjected to curfews and fury, became blazing hot. On one hand, the guardians of order had to assert their authority and their superior strength by boosting their firepower with truncheons and machine guns. On the other hand, they could not help but admire the courage of the protesters, their determination to counter their weapons bare-handed, to overthrow a government elected almost unanimously, to dare to march towards a new horizon. The police and the military had to resist prostrating themselves before the monk who maintained his lotus position while the match sizzled in contact with his gasoline-soaked robe until his body was totally consumed. One of the rare photographers who had not taken that day off immortalized the image of the monk become a human torch. Despite the unquestioned respect due to the monk's mental resolve, the immolation inspired lively debates about Buddhism and the desire to protect it from being sullied by politics.

Madame Nhu

Madame Nhu, sister-in-law to the South Vietnamese
president, and the most powerful woman in the country, sparked an outcry in the media when she used the word *barbecue* to describe the immolation. Erect and elegant in her traditional *áo dài*, which she had modernized by baring the neck and part of the shoulders, she had reproached the bonze for having failed in his independence, because he had used imported gasoline for his public suicide.

The guard at the Saigon Notre-Dame Cathedral sometimes let Louis sleep under the pews, on the cool tiled floor, when he needed shelter, if he'd been injured by a dog, a shard of glass, or a verbal insult. So it was that one day Louis was awakened by the sound of Madame Nhu's heels advancing towards the altar. She and her daughter were alone amid a group of men. Beneath the delicate lace square that hid part of her face, her gaze was piercing. Louis could not understand the orders given by Madame Nhu concerning the government's response to the upsurge of support for the Buddhists. But he knew instinctively that the nails of this woman with her doll's face, tiny body, and worldly exterior were the claws of a dragon, of a queen of the jungle. Instinctively, he pulled his legs back out of the beam of light and made himself small, even though he didn't know that Madame Nhu had formed an army of twenty-five thousand paramilitary women and that she had no qualms about brandishing a revolver at arm's length on a firing range in front of the cameras.

OPERATION BABYLIFT

One month before the tanks belonging to the Communist North Vietnamese Army rolled into the streets of Saigon, flying a new flag, one month before the last helicopter took off from the roof of the American embassy, one month before the victory of some and the defeat of others, President Gerald Ford freed up two million dollars to bring orphans born of American soldiers out of Vietnam. This was Operation Babylift.

The first aircraft chartered was a C-5 cargo plane, which was generally used to transport jeeps, shells, machine guns, and coffins. In the hold and the troop compartment, it contained babies lying directly on the floor or in boxes, well secured, for a short flight to Guam, the single stop before its final destination in the United States. The first orphans to arrive were settled on benches, sometimes two by two, and others under the seats. The photos show volunteers and soldiers securing the babies by any means available—striking visuals of innocent lives spawned by war. Of course, some among the older children, seated against the plane's walls, wept in the face of the unknown. But the other orphans had their eyes fixed on the chain of adults handing the babies along, while the very young were sound asleep in the armoured belly of the war machine.

Naomi descended from the plane after she had boarded her orphans. She was still on the tarmac when the aircraft exploded in flight. For a long time, many believed that the plane had been struck by enemy fire. The cause was, however, a simple breach, a mechanical fault that ripped away a door and the plane's tail. In an instant, the dreams of 78 children and 46 soldiers went up in smoke. At the very last moment the pilot was able to land the plane, on its back, in a rice paddy. Of the 314 on board, 176 survived.

One of the military rescuers recovered a body from the muddy ground that he thought was alive, because he saw no wound or scrape. Forty years later, he still remembered the exact moment when he raised it up. His eyes saw a sleeping baby with the skin intact, but his fingers felt as though they were holding a sack of marbles. This contradiction triggered an explosion inside his head and blasted his heart into a thousand pieces, like the bones of the baby.

The next day, on the same tarmac, Naomi climbed aboard a new aircraft with more orphans and the 176 survivors of the crash.

As for the orphans burned or asphyxiated by the depressurization, their ashes were buried in Thailand. Their lives came to an end in an unknown foreign country, mirroring the phrase that identified them when they were alive: *bụi đời* ("dust of life").

Naomi and the Orphans

When Naomi had learned that President Ford was putting Operation Babylift into effect, she left her own five-day-old baby with her family in Montreal to return at once to Saigon. The children in the orphanage she'd founded were waiting for her to save them.

Naomi was able to rent a *xe lam* to transport a dozen children to the airport. The *xe lam* has three wheels, with a motor that permits it to pull an open cabin. It usually accommodates a dozen passengers, or twice the number reckoned on by the manufacturer, Lambretta. Since it is public transport, the vehicle stops on demand, long enough for the passengers to hop on and grab a handhold or sit on someone's knees. On the way to the airport that day, people on the street jostled one another to get on board as well. They took the children into their arms, wanting to sit on one of the two benches positioned face to face. Naomi screamed, but no one paid heed to her. Each one tried to tell the driver their destination while holding out money, which lengthened the route and delayed Naomi's arrival with the children.

The *xe lam* driver helped Naomi carry the children to the tarmac, and into the plane. He tucked one baby's foot back into his box and reassured another infant, who yanked his old shirt so hard that she ripped it.

Naomi also had to find a place for herself on the plane, the first flight of Operation Babylift, which was to be greeted on its arrival in the United States by journalists and President Ford in person. On takeoff and landing, the orphans were surrounded by cameras and their blinding flashbulbs. While Naomi busied herself seating the children and securing them to the sides and floor of the plane, with or without their cardboard boxes, a volunteer informed her that another plane would be leaving the next day. Naomi decided to disembark and to go and collect the other children for the second flight.

Back on the tarmac beside the *xe lam* driver, she saw the plane explode, a ball of fire rising up in the rice fields at the end of the runway.

A photographer captured the reflection of the flames in her eyes—she who had crossed three continents, an ocean, and twelve time zones to battle fate. She was a mother who took herself for God, she who wanted to project her children into the future, like a parent saving a child by throwing her from the balcony of a house in flames. But here, wanting them to fly on the wings of a giant eagle, she had burned them alive. Naomi thought she was sparing her children a hell on earth. She didn't imagine that hell could also be found in the sky. If she had spoken Vietnamese, she would have known that "Sky" is the seat of power of the supreme being, he who determines matters of life, of death, and the sentences to be served by those who have not known how to respect life.

Ông Trời

Mr. Sky, or Ông Trời, envisaged eighteen torments to be inflicted on people guilty of bad behaviour. Those who squandered rice had to eat a worm for every grain left at the bottom of the bowl. Those who stole another's wife, duped a child, treated good people badly, would be thrown into a giant vat of boiling oil. Those who dishonestly evaded censure would be forced to stand in front of a mirror and stare at themselves. In hell, punishments are clearly defined. On Earth, Ông Trời punishes without following any precise plan, and according to a variable timeline. As well, he doesn't bother laying out the reasons for the punishments. Because it cannot be explained why an eighteen-year-old soldier, an adolescent, has been ordered to gather into his arms, from the midst of young rice shoots and the debris of a charred airplane, mud-covered corpses, including that of a baby perfectly preserved. He'd never held a baby in his arms before this rescue mission. On this baby who showed no wound, not even a scratch, the soldier did not see the face of death, or perhaps his heart hoped so much to encounter life that he had blinded himself until his hands felt the broken bones. Thirty, forty years later, the sensation of lifting the limp body of this baby suddenly came back to him when he was lifting a sack of charcoal; when he was showing his two-year-old grandson a squirrel's nest; when he heard a woman say, "*My God! Trời ơi!*", the telephone pressed to her ear in front of a shelf of cereal boxes in the grocery store.

Naomi didn't have time to mourn the seventy-eight losses, because she had to bestow the possibility of life on orphans who were still alive.

In the end, three thousand children were awarded a new beginning in a new country with new parents. The soldiers and the volunteers who had bottle-fed them delivered the first children to the adoptive parents waiting for them on the tarmac in San Francisco.

Surrounded by volunteers, soldiers, parents, and babies, President Ford, rocking an infant in his arms, smiled benevolently for the cameras. He knew that the tired eyes of these children, usually ignored, were helping him to present one last glorious image of the United States before its definitive retreat from Vietnam. That is why he rolled out the red carpet to welcome this "dust of life."

BUNNY

During Operation Babylift, Hugh Hefner, the founder and publisher of *Playboy*, lent his private jet and his "bunnies" to facilitate the transport of orphan children from the centre for processing adoption requests in California to adoptive parents in Madison, New York City, Chicago, and beyond. The bunnies knew how to cajole the babies with the same charm they deployed to weaken men's knees.

Annabelle, Emma-Jade, and Howard

Just as in the random occurrence of births, em Hồng found herself held close to Annabelle, her neck, her perfume. The name Emma-Jade brings to mind Southern belles. It came to her in Hugh Hefner's private jet, surrounded by women of the Playboy family.

Annabelle and Howard decided to raise Emma-Jade in Savannah as if the child had no other past than the one they would put together for her.

In her creaseless dresses, Annabelle performs the role of spouse to Howard, the respected politician with carefully groomed hair and a soothing voice. Whatever the day and hour, Howard can count on an impeccable home, always ready to be photographed, to host a meeting or a reception. As well, he can count on Annabelle's faultless appearance alongside his own. While Annabelle is guaranteed the title of Mrs. Pratt. On television or the radio, Howard often uses the expression "my wife and I."

Some of their friends are of the opinion that

Emma-Jade has the chin and the gaze of her father, Howard, while others insist that she is the spitting image of Annabelle.

It goes without saying that Emma-Jade looks like her mother. Her hair is done by Annabelle's hairdresser. She wears the same dresses, adapted for a model child and an unattainable princess. She sits like Annabelle, knees touching and leaning slightly to the left. Following in her mother's footsteps, Emma-Jade joins the cheerleading squad, plays volleyball, basketball, and the piano. Annabelle devotes herself heart and soul to Emma-Jade. In gratitude, or rather out of a survival instinct, Emma-Jade is a perfect reproduction of her mother.

During the twenty years of their life together, there is no scandal, no controversy. Their daily life is eventless, almost amnesiac. The days, the months, the years add up and repeat themselves like the minutes on a watch, without a shadow of doubt touching them. No one could suspect that Annabelle had committed herself to supporting the political ambitions of Howard and that he, in exchange, protected her from her rich and influential parents, who had forced her to swear before God to preserve both her virginity until marriage and the family's respectability by ceasing to passionately love her best friend Sophia.

Annabelle and Monique

During the annual apple pie competition in the spacious garden of the Savannah History Museum, Annabelle was charmed by Monique's *tarte tatin*, the pie the jury judged to be "naked," indecent even, because of the apple quarters exposed in all their plumpness. After that first meeting, Annabelle and Monique spent their days cooking together, exposing Emma-Jade to salade niçoise, cassoulet, strawberries with Chantilly cream, ladyfingers, and her first words of French.

In Monique's presence, Annabelle became another person. The loud laughter, bursting out, enveloped the kitchen like the flour that flew freely as much through the air as onto the floor and their faces. Monique told thousands of stories without worrying about making mistakes in English, gesticulating constantly to mime the taste of fresh butter from Normandy on the tip of the tongue, the height of her father, a giant, or the gait of her first boyfriend. The clinking of Monique's many rings when she held Emma-Jade's face to kiss her could make porcelain figurines come to life and dance, just as Annabelle did in her starched and belted dresses. During the Monique era, Annabelle was happy. Sublime.

A new work contract for Laurent, Monique's husband, took them to Montreal, the city Emma-Jade had chosen for her first foreign exchange, a city where she heard her friends talk about the music of the sand in the desert, the goddess Shakti, the aurora borealis . . . It was in Montreal too that she stopped visiting the hairdresser every month and no longer played the role of the blonde ingenue Brigitte Bardot, the discreet blonde Ingrid Bergman, the icy blonde Grace Kelly. Beneath the banal, anonymous, and natural brown of her hair, Emma-Jade saw her own face reveal itself, week by week, in the slightly almond shape of her eyes and in her golden complexion. People meeting her for the first time thought she was Brazilian, Lebanese, Siberian. All at once, she seemed to have come from somewhere far off, with no very precise identity.

After Montreal, Emma-Jade never went back to live in Savannah, and neither did Howard and Annabelle, who had settled in Washington. Emma-Jade roamed through several European universities, taking on jobs with no particular goal, until the one proposed to her by William.

William

William offered his clients virtual spaces where the rules were set by fantasy and love, by gambling. His fortune grew in rhythm with his subscribers' secret desires, their longing to watch women with extremely long armpit hair wrestle in mud; or to follow someone whose ambition, at the age of twenty-five, was to become the heaviest woman in the world by force-feeding herself through a funnel; or to watch a woman sleeping with a powered hair dryer on her pillow as she chewed on squares of toilet paper. William was also one of the first to create virtual dating sites, where love is divided into several groups and subgroups. After a doctorate in psychology and several years as a practising social worker, William knew the human animal inside out. Above all, he'd learned how to spy on it from a distance, just as he spied on his clients.

Every year, he hired an academic whose work consisted of opening up the world to him like an encyclopedia, in the way his father the log driver brought with him one book at a time to read at night at work sites in the woods, quoting to his fellow workers the next morning, and to his children when he was back home six months later. William thought Kool-Aid was something to help out "coolies"—he was still a young boy when his father compared the work of men in the bush to that of labourers in another age.

William and Emma-Jade

Since William no longer left his penthouse, he'd hired Emma-Jade to travel the world and give him reports on the conference in Finland that discussed the freeing up of millenary viruses and bacteria caused by the melting of the polar ice caps; on the work, under a microscope, of a passport forger; on the daily life of a woman who was afraid to touch buttons. Emma-Jade also relayed to him unprompted stories, anecdotes about people she met by chance as she moved from place to place.

The story that led William to sponsor a school in Cambodia came about when Emma-Jade met a taxi driver who had survived the Khmer Rouge after he had witnessed the decapitation, one after the other, of his teacher father and his brother, who was thought to be an intellectual because he wore glasses. During the two years the driver spent in the Cambodian forest with a group of adolescents separated from their parents by the soldiers, his only article of clothing was a pair of boxer shorts. At the end of the Pol Pot era, he had been able to find his mother and his six brothers and sisters, who had been dispersed to the four corners of the country; the youngest were seven and eight years old. Despite the family's flight to Paris, despite the lingering trauma of a blow to the head from a shovel intended to kill, he returned regularly to Cambodia, in the belief that love was to be found there, still.

Thanks to her conversation with her physicist neighbour on a train, Emma-Jade learned that researchers worked on unknown knowns, but also on unknown unknowns, because there was both the unknowable and the impossible. This meeting helped her to understand William better, and also to join that group of insatiables who believe that knowledge is the only semblance of the infinite that is accessible to humans. So it was that William renewed Emma-Jade's contract for an indefinite period. He hoped to keep his eyes on the world through those of Emma-Jade.

Emma-Jade

Emma-Jade hopscotched from one time zone to another. She flew over them without keeping track. She often lived thirty-hour days when she made leaps in time, her watch indicating the same hour more than once. Such flights enabled her to marvel at magnolias in flower several times in the same year. In a single autumn she gathered up and compared maple leaves fallen in Bremen, Kyoto, and Minneapolis.

She was one of those types of traveller who prompted airports to transform themselves into living environments. It was not unusual to find a grand piano and a pianist playing, with the same world-weariness, Beethoven and Céline Dion, thus ennobling to some degree the burgers and sushi served on plastic trays. Some airports featured libraries bathed in warm light and peaceful prayer rooms where believers could converse with the gods before placing themselves in the hands of technology once embarked. Some terminals positioned chaise longues in front of outsized windows flooded with sun, or massage chairs facing luxuriant plants from five continents, the roots of some entwining the young shoots of others. Ferns from Asia, begonias from South America, African violets, grew side by side cheerfully and abundantly, reassuring travellers who wanted to maintain contact with the outside world. The length of endless corridors, restaurant islands surged into view like oases. No menu adhered to culinary geography. Marinated olives were a stone's throw from Nordic salmon, while pad Thai faced off against fish and chips and *jambon-beurre*. The truly chic offered caviar and champagne, so you could celebrate your solitary birthday with bubbles and passing travellers.

You needed a trained eye to pick out Emma-Jade from the crowd. She always wore the same sweater in grey cashmere, a wool both light and warm. In her drawer, three identical pullovers lay in wait to replace the one whose stitches were being worn away by the friction from her shoulder straps and the weight of accumulated kilometres. The sweater protected her from the seats imprinted by the bodies of travellers who had preceded her. It was her refuge, her home away from home.

As usual, she had a snack before embarking, to help her fall asleep as soon as she settled into her seat, before takeoff, and before being assaulted by the scent of the lady who had tried out too many perfumes in the duty-free boutique, and that of the gentleman who had raced between two terminals in his overly heavy coat.

Emma-Jade and Louis

That day, Louis was the first passenger to rise and present himself at the open boarding gate. He had the standard look of a professional traveller: a steel-grey suitcase, charcoal pants, a lightweight black jacket, stretchy and close-fitting. Everything dark, discreet, almost invisible. In an instant, Emma-Jade knew that Louis would greet his neighbours with courtesy in order to keep them at bay and avoid any possible conversation. Like her, he slept as often above the clouds as he did on earth. Like her, he slept as comfortably sitting in the cramped space of numbered seats as bedded down in rooms with numbered doors.

She hurried to position herself second in line, behind him. She saw his passport already open at the proper page, which indicated that he knew how to insert his suitcase correctly in the luggage compartment without unduly blocking the aisle.

Emma-Jade felt a certain pride at being dressed like

a professional traveller, like Louis. She gripped the handle of her suitcase with her left hand, ready to move at the first crackling from the loudspeakers. Whatever the country or the airport, the voice announcing the flights always had the same intonation, the same rhythm, the same pace. She felt impatient to hear the beginning of the recording the agents used to announce the start of the flight. She was eager to sit back in her seat and fall asleep before takeoff. She couldn't wait to find herself in that constricted universe where she felt she was in her own little world, while at her side her neighbour's sigh would stir the air, an elbow on the armrest would inevitably be grazing hers, and she would recognize the film he'd chosen to view. But her seatmate would surely hear the tears inside her throat while she slept. The smell of the plane, the confinement of the passengers, and the constant noise of the engines each time induced a dull trembling in her stomach and an irresistible desire to sleep deeply, almost as if she were fainting.

At the signal, Louis and Emma-Jade stepped forward in unison, she behind him. They walked with the same rhythm, in sync with the steady noise of their wheeled luggage. They moved with assurance, obeying the rules, like soldiers on a military parade in the narrow corridors that rule out any discourtesy. They followed each other closely, keeping a polite distance, according to the unwritten laws of seasoned travellers.

Emma-Jade's life had always resembled these passageways that allowed you to move ahead without calling anything into question. On this day, though, Louis abruptly turned around at a display rack at a bend in the corridor. Just as he was avoiding a collision between his suitcase and Emma-Jade's foot, their eyes met, thereby putting a mark on this anonymous space. They might perhaps have stopped in their tracks, but the crowd behind them didn't allow it. They moved forward again, Emma-Jade three steps behind Louis.

Inside the plane, by the purest and happiest coincidence, only one seat separated them. Louis smiled at the flight attendant, talked to a passenger overloaded with bags, and greeted his neighbour. Emma-Jade retrieved the scarf that had fallen from its owner's shoulders, rounded by the passing of time. She handed their mutual neighbour her seat belt. They did not exchange words. But they looked at each other often, and at length.

For the first time in her life, Emma-Jade stayed awake, fascinated by the perfectly erect posture adopted by Louis during his sleep, despite his relaxed muscles.

On arrival, as Louis found himself behind Emma-Jade in the line for passport control, she approached and offered him the photo she'd taken of him.

Louis, Tâm, and Isaac

100 Emma-Jade saw Louis again for the first time in Bordeaux, in response to the invitation written on page 122 of W.G. Sebald's *Austerlitz*, a novel she'd been reading during the plane trip. Then they met in Guam, an island in the Pacific Ocean halfway between Japan and Australia, east of the Philippines, and west of the ocean's vastness. Louis had landed there as a refugee child, and there he had become the son of Tâm and Isaac, lost in the midst of seventeen thousand feet of fencing on the American air force base, with its four hundred dry toilets and three-quarters of the entire B-52 fleet. Tâm had been the interpreter for Isaac, a historian from Montreal obsessed with the fate of the first Vietnamese exiles—he fell instantly in love with her. She had also been one of the interpreters of the confused and anxious words of a hundred thousand Vietnamese who'd had the good fortune to find refuge in Guam after April 30, 1975, after the loss of their Vietnam.

HELICOPTER

Of all the helicopters that landed in the midst of the shooting to rescue wounded soldiers and collect mangled corpses, the most famous rotations were those at dawn between April 29 and 30, 1975, aircraft loaded with civilians who'd succeeded in scaling walls. The Saigonese ran towards the port and in particular towards the American embassy in the hope of escaping the tanks arriving from the North to proclaim the peace. The privileged ones knew that there were twenty-eight other evacuation points, including thirteen roofs identified with a large *H*, the exact dimensions of the Huey helicopters' landing pad. Some shrewd individuals offered jewels or their motorcycles to the chauffeurs of high-ranking Americans so they would be told where to run to, how to escape the city now encircled by the new occupiers.

For nine hours, Saigon's sky formed the backdrop for a choreography of helicopters transformed into evacuation shuttles. In order to maximize the capacity of the available Hueys and the number of takeoffs and landings, the military did not respect the rules: there was only one pilot per copter, and crucially, they allowed twenty to twenty-four people on board instead of twelve, the number deemed safe. During one of the last takeoffs, an American chose to fly standing up on the landing skids, clinging to the machine gun, in order to give up his place to a young boy on his own and two children held out to him by their parents, who remained at the bottom of the ladder. At dusk, the helipads improvised on tennis courts and the ambassador's parking lot were lit by the headlights of cars grouped in a circle.

Those responsible for Operation Frequent Wind moved heaven and earth so that thirty-one volunteer pilots could save 978 Americans and 1,220 Vietnamese and other nationalities from the American embassy alone. Among the evacuees, one teenaged girl became a biotechnology researcher in Georgia, a young man built a career as an anaesthetist in California, and another made a fortune on fish in Texas.

Louis and Saigon

As Louis was sleeping with his ear pressed to the ground,
he heard police moving about, as well as ambassadors, company directors, and secret service agents, but also the sound of the rebels' naked feet. No one suspected that, beneath the three-metre-wide house of the woman who bought and sold used glass and cardboard, a cell of resisters was preparing the overthrow of the government in power. Louis was one of the few people to have noticed the air hole hidden under the wooden bench where the merchant sat all day. Had they been able, like him, to blot out the noises—of bottles being weighed, the handling of bundles of newspapers, scooter and bicycle horns—passersby would have heard voices discussing the seizure of the radio station; the transfer of money to the North; the advance of troops towards the South; the victorious peace that would soon emerge as soldiers fell at the front and citizens were taken hostage between two lines of fire.

The city of Saigon was not sitting on a volcano about

to erupt. Its nervousness derived not from the streets thronged with sellers of feather dusters, from women perched on their high heels, from the jeeps of MPs, but rather from deep roots forcing upwards the asphalt and mud, from dust and identities being beaten down.

Louis sensed the earthquake approaching beneath his feet. On the sidewalks, he heard chauffeurs placing bets among themselves on the scope of the coming bloodbath. Employers forgot that their chauffeurs, backs turned and silent behind the wheel, picked up their words despite themselves. Foreign words at first, that with time form sentences revealing the most deeply hidden secrets, the cruellest desires, and the most sensitive information. During a conversation between the oil company director's wife and her tourist friend, the chauffeur caught a remark: *The temperature in Saigon is 105 and rising*; the lawyer's chauffeur heard his employer teach his son how to recognize and whistle "White Christmas"; the engineer's learned from his daughter that the signal to evacuate would be given on the radio; the chauffeur for the director of the Vietnam–United States friendship club, *Việt Mỹ*, spotted the roofs that would serve as heliports on D-Day. While there was no official association of chauffeurs, they would inevitably meet up around coffee kiosks to wait for their employers. It would have taken just a few exchanges for them to piece together the evacuation plan from bits of information collected, positioned, and understood like pieces of a puzzle.

The final month before the definitive American retreat from Vietnam, fewer and fewer Americans were circulating in the streets of Saigon and visiting the go-go bars.

Like Louis, Tâm also sensed the city's secret trembling. One of her besotted clients advised her to listen to the radio, alert for the top secret signalling of the end and the withdrawal.

It was hard to contain the panic, as seats on commercial airlines became harder and harder to find, and departures more and more numerous.

When a military plane exploded in the air, right after takeoff, the tension abruptly shot up a notch. The Saigonese didn't know that this plane was carrying not tanks or soldiers or sophisticated weapons, but orphans.

Louis

106 He followed the chauffeurs who responded, along with their bosses, to the “White Christmas” signal broadcast on the radio. Making his way through the mass of adults, he arrived at the roof where people were climbing one by one up the ladder to the hovering helicopter, with the help of an American official. Louis was able to climb up in his place thanks to the indecency of a man who had passed in front, jostling the whole line. The official swiftly drew the man away from the ladder’s steps before putting him out of commission with a powerful punch underneath the whirring blades and the deafening noise of the rotor. Louis always believed he took the place of that man on the ground, abandoned on the roof, because even the person in charge had to exit the platform and stand on the aircraft’s landing skid.

Louis and 6,967 other evacuees were set down on ships chartered for this mission, Operation Frequent Wind.

Perhaps his father was none other than the man

who landed the last helicopter in the embassy's landing space to save the eleven Marines *in extremis,* forgotten by Operation Frequent Wind.

Perhaps.

Tâm and the *Tiger*

There were many helicopter round trips above the American embassy, which Tâm had managed to enter.

The end of the war arrived noisily, as if peace had to be proclaimed and welcomed with gunshots, fires, howling, and panic attacks.

The American ambassador received the order to leave, to proceed with the evacuation. All those who knew that persecution awaited them at the hands of the victors converged on the embassy, while the employees shredded and burned telegrams, banknotes, secret documents. The traffic lights, just like the policemen standing at intersections, baton in hand, under their umbrella-shaped metal shelters, were totally ignored by the constant flow of vehicles. Just like animals that smell the beginnings of an earthquake, the people ran, seeking a place to find refuge from the columns of tanks and military trucks advancing proudly, the soldiers brandishing the new flag.

Outside the embassy, the demarcation between sidewalks

and streets was worn away. People crowded against the barricaded doors, guarded by submachine guns that were ready and nervous, and against the entrances to buildings leading to the rooftops, to the ladders, to the platforms of other helipads from where they hoped to be taken towards the open sea. Towards the vastness of the unknown.

Just like the helicopter that transported Louis, that of Tâm landed on one of the crowded ships. There were also people who arrived on board by way of small craft. They climbed up ropes and chains. Some lost their footing, others let go and plunged. Tâm saw soldiers tipping helicopters overboard to make more room for the evacuees. The soldiers ignored the maximum capacity for security and the regulation number of flight hours. The pilots had doubled the number of flights possible by leaving their co-pilots at the command of other helicopters. One by one, they turned in the sky until late, until dark, until the last opportunity, knowing that hundreds of people congregated around the embassy swimming pool were still hoping for another flight, another last flight.

The official end of Operation Frequent Wind was communicated to the soldiers by the signal *"Tiger, tiger, tiger."* Or was it rather, *"Tiger is out"*? One thing is certain, as of that moment, the noise of tanks on asphalt replaced that of rotors in the sky.

NAIL POLISH

Humans belong to that category of animals characterized by ninety-five percent of the body being just one colour. They cannot spread their feathers, nor sweep the ground with their tails, nor inflate a gular sac in order to seduce or to ward off. And so they dress up, put on makeup, and colour their nails. From the warriors of Babylon, who blackened their nails, to Cleopatra, who dipped her fingers into red henna, through to the Chinese imperial family, which favoured the brilliance of gold and silver; princes distinguished themselves from their subjects by forbidding them to use their sacred colours.

We had to wait for the invention of the automobile before the adornment of nails was democratized. At the beginning of the twentieth century, the sheen of automobile paint and nail polish seduced the bourgeois and encouraged the middle class to aspire to riches. Since then, bottles of lacquer have lined the shelves of department stores and nail salons, and found a place in makeup kits. Even though the industry targets only half the population, it generates eight billion dollars a year. In laboratories, chemists spend even their weekends wrestling with the fragility of materials and with nails that grow and grow again without stopping, covered or not with a piece of acrylic, embellished or not. Scientists cannot overcome reality: nature goes her own way and shows herself to be transparent, neutral, without intent.

In beauty salons, manicurists propose an almond shape to replace the square of the natural nail, and vaunt the shiny over the matte to allow their clients to re-enter their lives' arenas while subduing their current troubles: the sequined glaze shines for those who do not see the end of the tunnel; turquoise pleases those who are enduring turmoil; pointed nails are favoured by those who have been clawed. On their YouTube channels, enthusiasts invent new trends with the help of images that hold out the promise of a virtual paradise or an outrageous youth. Many explain and show how to file, clean, cut, glue, trim, and varnish. Step by step, alone for long minutes in front of the camera, they address an audience that is equally alone on the other side of the screen.

In a little more than a century, the palette of colours has been augmented with hundreds of nuances. The name of each asserts a singularity designed to reinforce the mood of she who wears it: Butterfly Kisses for pink cotton candy or daddy's girl; Prêt-à-Surfer for the ocean blue of open waters; Mad Women for audacious raspberry velvet; Sunday Funday for coral innocence; Crème Brûlée for static beige; Lincoln Park After Dark for the grey of sleepless nights; Funny Bunny for stolen innocence; Devil's Own Red for fatal blood, oxidized.

Louis created Rice Paddy Green, Bottle Green, Guava Green, to parse the colour of em Hồng's eyes.

Tâm, Isaac, and Louis

Isaac married Tâm and adopted Louis on the soil of Guam. Together, they formed a family that made passersby frown, or smile.

On the fifth anniversary of the formation of their family, Isaac took Tâm and Louis to California, to trace the progress of those Vietnamese whom he'd seen pass through Guam. To his great surprise, he found that most of the refugees who'd become immigrants had settled well into their new lives, and that a good number of them owned their own businesses—a little restaurant, a commercial house-cleaning company, a specialized food store, or an insurance agency. But nail salons were the most common of all.

During her visit to a camp in 1975, Tippi Hedren, the actress in the Alfred Hitchcock film *The Birds*, received compliments from the Vietnamese refugees for her impeccable fingernails, which gave her the idea of organizing a manicure class for twenty or so women. Her first students, new Californians, passed their knowledge on to sixty more, who themselves trained other manicurists, and so they multiplied, becoming three hundred and sixty, three thousand and sixty, and more. In only a few years, they had opened nail salons all over the United States, in Europe, and throughout the world.

Tâm opened her first salon in Montreal after receiving advice from Thuân, who had never made any comments in Guam about Tâm's mixed blood or that of Louis.

Thuân was the first Vietnamese to join forces with Olivett, owner of an Afro-American hairdressing salon in the Los Angeles neighbourhood of South Bay. Lowering her prices by sixty to seventy-five percent, she offered her services to the Olivett clientele. Their partnership gave rise to new needs, a new culture, and a new business, which today is worth eight billion American dollars—or the price of 48,484 used Huey helicopters; or six return trips between the sun and Earth in kilometres; or the mass of 5,525 Boeing 747-400s in kilograms; or eight times the billion iPhones sold. If Vietnamese women's own tastes were close to those of bourgeois white women, who prefer shapes and colours that are classic and conservative, the Vietnamese manicurists quickly adapted to the expressive, striking, extravagant tastes of their Black clients, whose exuberant creativity finds expression right to the tips of their nails.

Isaac helped Tâm out at the opening of her salon, while Louis gave her a hand after school and on weekends, studying during bus rides and at night to keep up with his friends and catch up on the ten first years of his life when he'd been deprived of theories, schedules, rules.

Tâm did not have set opening or closing hours. She followed the rhythm of her clients: an appointment at dawn for those getting married, and at night for those with amorous rendezvous; and any time in between for those who came with a prescription from their psychologist or sex therapist, or who were preparing for a trip to the seaside.

As soon as Tâm was able to do so, she offered financial help to those of her employees who wanted to open their own salons. Louis helped those new owners to rent spaces, fix them up, expand and renew their inventory and their clientele. From year to year, he got more involved in the various aspects of a business whose growth was being spurred on by new discoveries and creations shared through pictures, through videos, and in conversations in the salons. He aided and abetted the dizzying growth of the Vietnamese community by criss-crossing the planet, both on the beaten track and along secondary roads.

Louis and the Manicures

Louis roamed the world because his success depended on the number of displays featuring the same flasks of nail polish, arranged in the same order, lit everywhere with the same light, from a village of five hundred people to a city with a population of ten million. From one nail salon to another, from one country to another, the same techniques were used, the same trends spread abroad, identical hands were held for hours without ever becoming acquainted.

The women installed on seats on casters close to the ground, their noses level with their clients' feet, almost all came from the same place, a place where the sun shone without offering them a brilliant future. There, they wore conical hats, covered their noses with handkerchiefs folded into triangles like those of cowboys from the Wild West, and they sold; they might sell newspapers, hats, or baguettes secured with strings to an improvised display case that would disintegrate at the slightest show of anger; they'd sell to passersby on the side of a dusty road; they'd sell so they might eat a bowl of rice at the end of the day. Or they could marry a foreigner from South Korea, Taiwan, or China, in exchange for a few thousand dollars that they would leave to their family, knowing well that this new husband would trade them in for another if they couldn't take care of the mother-in-law suffering from Alzheimer's or the paralyzed father-in-law, or if they didn't submit to the violence of conjugal duties. They would have the right to cry out in pain and wail at injustice on those distant islands, but their language would only be understood by the dunes or the eternal return of the tides. Or they could pay tens of thousands of dollars not to be touched by those men, in which case they would require a man who would agree to sign a marriage contract with them, in other words a document promising them a foreign country. Never mind where he came from, this ersatz husband innocent of love, they knew in advance that they could pay their debts by sanding down callused heels. Paring away the dead skin of each toe allowed them to lessen their fear of seeing themselves denounced by the make-believe husband and finding themselves without papers.

Louis knew the precarity of these women who chose beauty as their profession, and as an escape hatch. He crossed the planet from east to west, from north to south, in straight lines, in zigzags, in pas de deux, keeping them up to date on the marketing of new products, thanks to which they would never lack for work. The mode for squared-off nails, for very long artificial nails decorated with or without fake diamonds, fell in and out of fashion as rapidly and arbitrarily as nails pointed like lions' claws. He trained his clients to suggest the orbit manicure and the half-moon style between two waves of French manicures. Clear nails sat beside deepest black and banana yellow. These canvases of less than one square centimetre offered endless possibilities, as if all dreams could be found at one's fingertips.

The nail salons improved over the years. During the 1980s, when Louis visited a salon for the first time, there were no three-speed massage chairs over a whirlpool foot bath, no resin balls, or acrylic-based gel, or fibreglass. The clients were happy to have nails covered in polish perfectly applied; they could not aspire to a massage of the calves with hot stones or drying under an ultraviolet lamp. Thanks to Isaac, his adoptive father, the husband of his adoptive mother, Tâm, Louis discovered this universe in its infancy, when the Vietnamese were still largely in the minority. Today, they control half the market. According to statistics, they have held in their hands one-half of all the hands that have lacquered fingers.

Louis and Emma-Jade

Emma-Jade found Louis for the third time at the Saigon airport. As he was a head taller than most of the people in the crowd, he did not have to nudge anyone aside in order to be seen. Since the end of the war, every Vietnamese traveller arriving from abroad has been awaited by members of their extended family, gathering in great numbers because that signifies a "coming home" after a long absence. The families rent vans and fill them by order of priority. Whether there has been fifteen years, twenty years, or thirty years of separation, the family remains united: cousins, brothers and sisters, the new nephews and nieces, children, aunts and uncles, parents. It's a celebration. The family is a celebration. Unlike those visitors whose oversized suitcases and giant boxes overflow with Werther's caramels, LU biscuits, moisturizing creams, the latest in menstrual pads, Emma-Jade is, as usual, wheeling her simple carry-on.

Seated on the hotel terrace facing Louis, Emma-Jade

has fallen asleep despite the constant noise from the countless scooters, bicycles, and cars, just like em Hồng. Louis watches her sleep until she wakes twenty-four hours later, exactly as before.

Tâm and Emma-Jade

Tâm was able to be the mother of her newborn for no more than a few minutes after she had brought her into the world.

The midwife hired by her employer had handed the baby to a rickshaw driver as soon as she began to cry, so that Tâm could go right back to the go-go bar stage without having had time to give a name to her daughter, who subsequently received two first names: Hồng and Emma-Jade.

Tâm and Isaac

122 On her deathbed, Tâm asked to smell a bowl of *phở* and her last words were *"Isaac yêu."* She could have called him "darling," "honey," or "chéri," words she had heard so often from the mouths of soldiers. But it was the word *yêu*, that word of love with its deep roots, that best resonated when she was in Isaac's arms.

Just like the rubber tree leaves on the plantation of her father, Alexandre, Tâm died from the rainbow rain of herbicides that fell during her childhood. And perhaps also from nail polish, according to her oncologist.

PHỞ

No Vietnamese living in Vietnam makes *phở* broth at home. But every Vietnamese living outside Vietnam has prepared or eaten a homemade *phở* at least once, since expatriate Vietnamese can't just leave the house and go to a *phở* kiosk on the street corner. In Saigon, there are probably as many *phở* sellers as there are alleyways. Each counter differs according to the precise balancing of its recipe, according to the proportions of its various ingredients: *cinnamon, nutmeg, coriander seeds, star anise, cloves, ginger, oxtail, beef flank, beef bones, chicken bones, bavette, beef tendon, fish sauce, shallots, chopped onion, fresh coriander, culantro, Thai basil, bean sprouts, rice vermicelli, pepper, fresh chili pepper, pepper sauce.*

It's impossible to reproduce these broths at home, cooked in cauldrons that, for two or three decades, have been used to cook and to combine ingredients, an intimate space for slow exchanges, shy aromas, and the noblest of perfumes. If scientists were to make a close study of those vessels, they would find traces of their owners' taste buds—the cinnamon rising first from the cauldron of the woman on Hạ Hồi Street, while that of her neighbour was set apart by the burnt scent of grilled ginger. The variations number at least twenty-four to the power of twenty-four. Everyone has their favourite spot: friends exchange addresses, lovers are drawn to the first bowl they shared together, schoolchildren make their choices according to size and quantity. Families return, nostalgic, to the same place, generation after generation.

Once upon a time, Louis savoured the soups prepared to other clients' tastes. Nothing was wasted, because he grabbed the bowls as soon as the clients rose from their stools. If he didn't hurry, the waiters would pour what was left into a pail that went to the pigs. In time, he learned to recognize the clients by what was left of their soup. There was the one who always scented her *phở* with ten or fifteen basil leaves that she frantically tore from their stems while her sister emptied the plate of bean sprouts into her bowl. The bodybuilder client dropped a raw egg into the soup along with an extra ladle of fat. Louis became accustomed to pepper thanks to a very old woman who coloured her soup red. He always wondered whether the woman's eyesight had deteriorated or if her taste buds had become numb from her having spent so much time scolding people. The owner of the stall muttered that only the hugely jealous ate such hot spice.

Louis was the sum of all those clients.

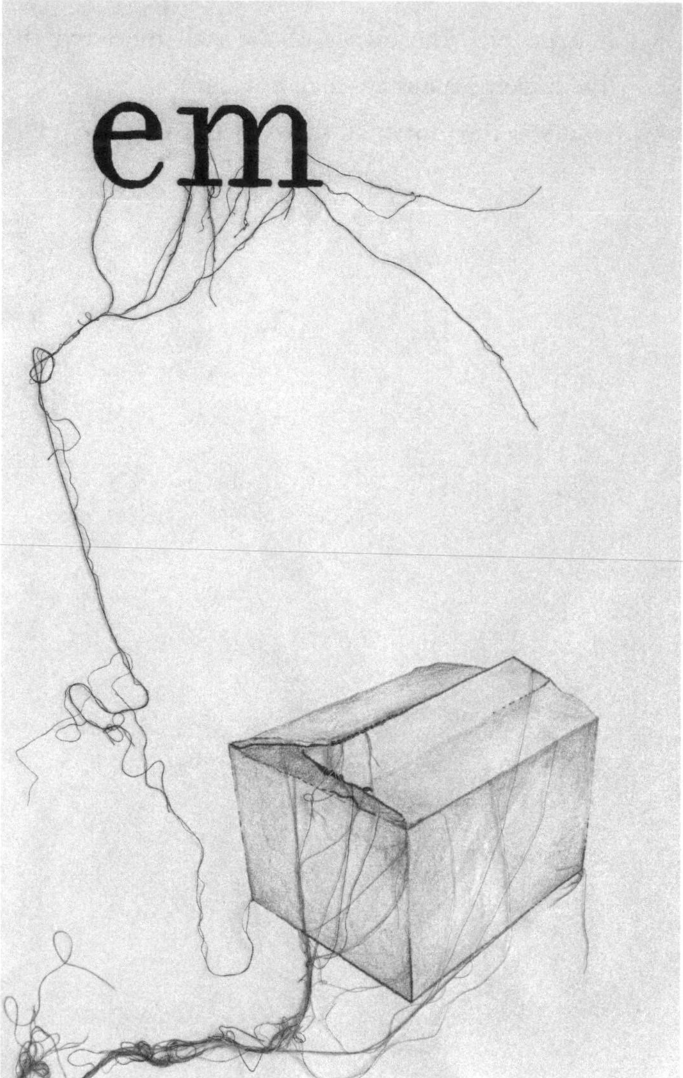

ART BY LOUIS BOUDREAULT

Truths without end

If I knew how to end a conversation, if I could distinguish true truths, personal truths from instinctive truths, I would have disentangled the threads for you before tying them up or arranging them so that the story of this book would be clear between us. But I have followed the advice of the painter Louis Boudreault, who advised me to play with the threads in the artwork he created for this book. Some threads stayed where they were despite the veering to the left and the ups and downs when the painting was moved from Monsieur Boudreault's studio to my home. Others imposed themselves by coming away from the canvas in the middle of the night, as I listened to the silences and testimonies of the soldiers, the combatants, and those who refused to fight; while I erased thousands of words in blocks, in paragraphs, in sentences, so as not to underscore some, to highlight others too boldly, and in the end to betray the delicate balance that maintains us in love. And in life.

I would have taken so much pleasure in describing for you the crown that Emma-Jade wore when she was the homecoming queen at school; in telling you what she chose as a tattoo ("What you seek is seeking you") for her shoulder blade; the positioning of her legs around Louis's waist when he carried her on his back to take her to bed.

I would also have liked to give you news of the family of John, the pilot who saved Tâm; of Naomi's daughter, Heidi, who has five Vietnamese brothers and sisters; of the aged My Lai survivor who invited the American soldiers to come back so she could forgive them.

I would have comforted you with examples of prisons transformed into tourist sites and "five-free" nail salons that contribute to the reduction of cancer by no longer using varnish containing formaldehyde, toluene, dibutyl phthalate, formaldehyde resin, and camphor.

I avoided saddening you with the soundtrack that reveals President Nixon's order to proceed with the bombardment despite the hesitation of the general who came to inform him that the sky was too overcast to avoid civilian casualties; and the document that presents the reasons for which the war had to go on:

1. 10% to support democracy;
2. 10% to support South Vietnam;

3. 80% to avoid humiliation.

I tried to interweave the threads, but they escaped, and remain unanchored, impermanent and free. They rearranged themselves on their own, given the speed of the wind, the news streaming by, the worries and smiles of my sons. The pages that follow constitute an imperfect ending, with scraps and figures drawn from life.

Louis and Emma-Jade in Saigon

I heard Louis describe his childhood neighbourhood to Emma-Jade:

"The nail you see there, it's been in that tree for at least forty years. The barber who set himself up on this bit of sidewalk hung his mirror there."

"Down this dark alley, there was a hundred-year-old or possibly immortal lady who brought her scale every morning and offered to read the weight of passersby. As well as the weight on their backs."

"My mother Tâm lived in this apartment."

"When I was young, I loved to listen to the music they played in this bar."

"That Pan Am sign has never been removed. I'm negotiating to buy it. It would be a memory of Pamela, who taught me to read, my first words in English."

"I stole tins of condensed milk from this kiosk to feed you. The owner was still alive and working when I returned twenty years later to pay for them. She remembered me. What's more, she knew."

I see Emma-Jade and Louis lying on the ground, their heads under the pink granite bench that had been their common home, the place where Emma-Jade had landed after the rickshaw driver had taken her away with him. That day, the explosion in the open-air bar facing the park had wounded many and killed one, a rickshaw driver who had gone to return a briefcase left behind by a soldier client.

Howard, Annabelle, and Emma-Jade

132 Howard and Annabelle joined Emma-Jade in Saigon to be with her and explain that they had concealed her origins because of the exaggerated and contradictory feelings towards veterans like Howard, once they returned and resumed ordinary life within their community, in their own country.

RAINBOW

The rainbow represents hope, joy, perfection. And yet, the word *rainbow* was chosen to designate the herbicides poured down on Vietnam, those substances that caused the cancer of Tâm, who as a child had seen leaves falling from the plantation trees as if autumn had crept between the seasons of heat and of monsoons. Imagine what there was:

- 20,000 flights flown;
- 20,000,000 gallons of defoliants and herbicides, or more than 80,000,000 litres spilled widely, as from a storm;
- 20,000 square kilometres contaminated, that is to say, beyond the horizon line, beyond the foot of Mr. Sky;
- 24 percent of Vietnamese territory sprayed with these rainbow colours;
- 3,000,000 human beings poisoned and at least 9,000,000 near and dear to them in mourning;

- 1,000,000 congenital malformations as proof of human genius.

Operation Ranch Hand, which lasted from 1961 to 1971, had as its goal to make foliage wither away, exposing the enemy. Subsequently, more powerful products infiltrated the earth and burned out roots. The most effective desiccated the earth, preventing seeds from growing back. You would have thought that life had been eradicated. Yet humans resisted and survived, accepting the presence of these poisons that are now part and parcel of what they are.

The dioxins are still there, generations later. These toxic products have contaminated genes, have blended with chromosomes, have worked their way into cells. They have formed and deformed in their image, the image of all-powerful man.

Contrary to what its name implies, Agent Orange, as a defoliant, was closer to pink or brownish.

The child who saw the planes flying side by side to spray the ground with that herbicide would have thought it was an air show. In four minutes, a C-123 spilled its stock, three cubic metres of Agent Orange per square kilometre, over sixteen kilometres of forest. Even if the planes were escorted by a helicopter equipped with a machine gun and by a fighter plane, the operation was still dangerous because the trees died only after two or three weeks. On the ground, the camouflaged enemy waited, weapons pointed towards the sky, prepared to die now or fifteen or twenty years later, from liver cancer, heart disease, or melanoma.

The child, witness to the deafening dance of the planes, could not have made the connection between the trail of mist and the leaves falling, freed by the winds, as in love songs. He might have thought that the tropical forest, which had known only the rotation of dry and wet seasons, had miraculously been visited by autumn, that season of sweet melancholy, season of an imagined Occident.

Despite its effectiveness, Agent Orange did not stop the rice from growing. It had been preceded by other agents: green, pink, purple. After it, chemists invented the white and the blue. Each variety was identified by a coloured band painted right onto the barrel. Each colour had as its function to defoliate, clear underbrush, or uproot. Together, they constituted the rainbow herbicides of Operation Ranch Hand. Their primary mission was to obliterate the wealth of the tropical forest, then to starve the enemy by purging harvests. Most of the trees were killed on first contact. The most tenacious gave up after the second or third exposure. But the rice resisted. Whatever the colour of the agent, it was almost impossible to burn it. Even grenades and mortar fire in the rice paddies could not make it vanish entirely. The seeds grew back, continued to feed the resisting soldiers as well as the farmers who found themselves in the wrong place at an abhorrent moment in history. Agent Blue had to be invented in order to dry out the soil, thus depriving the rice of its principal source of life, water. Agent Blue triumphed over the rice.

Operation Ranch Hand might have been celebrated as a military strategy had there not been all those American soldiers who were also affected by the herbicides. Gravitational force was supposed to draw the drops downwards, towards the enemy. But the winds intervened, and the sprayers were also sprayed.

The children who were lucky enough to grow old saw in ten years eighty million litres of rainbow-coloured herbicides manufacture rain in the midst of fine weather.

Today, forty-five years later, those children's children's countless grave congenital deformities confirm the power of humans to mutate genes, to alter nature, to hoist themselves to the rank of gods. We have the power to generate a face that is halfway melted; to grow a second skull larger than the first; to coax eyes out of their sockets; to empty the soul of its breath of life by pouring down tanks of liquid pink as flowers, white as nonchalance, purple as purple hearts, green as leaves under the monsoon rains, and blue as the boundless sky.

The Forgotten

- 8,744,000 military personnel participated in the war involving the United States, North Vietnam, and South Vietnam;
- 58,177 American soldiers were killed, and 153,303 wounded;
- 1.5 million military personnel and 2 million civilians died in North Vietnam;
- 255,000 military personnel and 430,000 civilians were killed in South Vietnam.

I wonder why there are only round figures on one side and exact ones on the other, and above all, why no list included the number

- of orphans;
- of widows;
- of aborted dreams;
- of broken hearts.

I also wonder if all those figures would have been different had love been considered in the calculations, the strategies, the equations, and above all the battles.

VIETNAM, APRIL 30, 1975

A country shaped like an *S*, perhaps echoing its tortuous history, or its grace. Its slender waist, only fifty kilometres wide, connects brothers and sisters who see themselves as enemies. Yet they fought the Chinese together on the backs of elephants for thousands of years. Then rose up together against France for a hundred years. Their victory was debated and negotiated for so long around a table in Geneva that people fell asleep while waiting to celebrate the agreement.

By the time they awoke, the country was split in two, as in a cellular division. Each part evolved on its own side, and the two of them rediscovered each other twenty years later, reunited and transformed. Angry. The North had sacrificed like a big brother to free its South, which had been taken hostage by the United States. The South lamented the loss of its freedom to dance to the music of the Doors, to read *Paris Match*, to work for Texaco. Out of benevolence, and by redistributing powers, the North severely punished the South for having succumbed to the charm and the power of America. The South went quiet, fled during moonless nights, while the North padlocked the borders, the doors, and speech.

After forty-five years of shared day-to-day life under the same flag, the delicate waist at the centre of the country still bears the scar of the incision imagined by politics. This old wound is so deep, so muted, that it has spread beyond the territory. Whether the Vietnamese meet in Dakar, Paris, Warsaw, New York, Montreal, Moscow, or Berlin, they still introduce themselves in terms of their starting point: Northerner or Southerner; pro- or anti-American; they identify themselves as before or after 1954, before or after 1975.

In 2025, April 30 will be a Wednesday, as it was in 1975. The fiftieth anniversary will certainly be a great event for all Vietnamese. But it will doubtless be observed separately and differently from one group to another. On one side, Vietnam will on that date celebrate the reunification of North and South everywhere in the country. On the other side, on that day, the Vietnamese who fled after April 30, 1975, will mourn the fall of Saigon in Sydney, Austin, San Jose, Vancouver, Paris, Frankfurt, Montreal, Tokyo . . .

This fiftieth anniversary will confirm in all likelihood

that memory is a faculty of forgetfulness. It forgets that all Vietnamese, no matter where they live, descend from a love story between a woman of the immortal race of fairies and a man of the blood of dragons. It forgets that their country was surrounded by barbed wire that transformed it into an arena and that they found themselves adversaries, forced to fight each other. Memory forgets the distant hands that pulled the strings and the triggers. It only remembers the blows, the aching pain of those blows that bruised roots, snapped ancestral bonds, and destroyed the family of immortals.

AN IMAGINARY CONVERSATION WITH TIM O'BRIEN

TIM O'BRIEN: *A bullet can kill the enemy, but a bullet can also produce an enemy, depending on whom that bullet strikes.*

KIM: *Toute balle qui tue un ennemi en crée au moins un autre. Peu importe la personne touchée.*

Any bullet that kills an enemy creates at least one more. No matter who is the person struck.

A LUNAR CONVERSATION WITH THE PAINTER LOUIS BOUDREAULT

KIM: *It goes without saying that this box is amazing. My heart skips a beat, for two reasons: the box itself and you. Do you think one can die from too much beauty?*

LOUIS BOUDREAULT: *One should die only from beauty. When I have finished it, we will know on seeing it that it contains the inexpressible.*

KIM: *All these threads of life as time goes by*
All these threads without knots without ties to trace the life-line of the abandoned
All these threads patiently embroidered that allow tightrope walkers to cross through life in equilibrium
All your threads

LOUIS BOUDREAULT: *You would think that a breath might undo it, but if it resists nothing will be able to destroy it . . .*

And it resisted.

COLD WAR

146 A conflict between East and West that crystallized in a war between the North and the South of Vietnam, on either side of the Seventeenth Parallel, from 1954 to 1975. The war devolved from the Geneva Accords, an armistice treaty that put an end to French Indochina (Laos, Cambodia, and Vietnam).

The Accords were signed in Switzerland in 1954 by two parties, the French Republic and North Vietnam, led by Ho Chi Minh. In the attempt to undo the links, the ties, and the customs joining France and Vietnam, among others, the negotiations lasted almost two months, around a table with representatives of several countries:

- China
- the Soviet Union
- Laos
- Cambodia
- North Korea

- South Korea
- the United Kingdom
- France
- North Vietnam
- Poland
- India
- Canada
- the United States.

As in a play, the doors opened and slammed to intimidate some and to support others, or to test the position of each while trying to manoeuvre oneself closer or farther away. The players bargained by detaching a territory here, shifting a border there, in latitude or longitude, adding an entitlement to military presence, promising autonomy, or independence, trading off their convictions for the prospect of a new alliance. They modified the geopolitical map of the region, endowing it with a leopard skin motif, the same as that of the rubber and coffee plantations. The discussions had been so bitter and the stakes so complex and critical that the negotiators forgot the existence of simple human beings, the ones waiting on those lands for the arrival of a baby or the ripening of a mango or, on a school bench, the announcement of a grade.

As a result of all the compromises that bore with

them counterfeit and contradictory promises, a new war saw the light of day between the North and the South of Vietnam. This war lasted twenty years because Vietnam had suddenly gained in importance on the international scene. It became a point of contention in the balance of power between China, the USSR, and the United States. After some twenty years of staring each other down without daring to blink, the three great powers decided to alter the game and the dance. They shook hands in front of the cameras, which left the hands of Vietnam empty and without a partner. That is how Vietnam lost its strategic importance and its place on the chessboard.

Their abandonment by the three great powers forced the two Vietnams to find themselves, to live together despite the discomfort. The tears of rage and bewilderment, of hatred and victory, of fatigue and joy, blended with the picture of brothers and sisters who must awkwardly embrace after a long dispute, while their hearts were still bleeding and their bodies covered in bruises. Under those conditions, peace was officially proclaimed on April 30, 1975.

Born in Saigon in 1968, KIM THÚY left Vietnam with the boat people at the age of ten and settled with her family in Quebec. A graduate in translation and law, she has worked as a seamstress, interpreter, lawyer, restaurant owner, media personality and television host. She lives in Montreal and devotes herself to writing. Kim Thúy has received many awards, including the Governor General's Literary Award in 2010, and was one of the top four finalists of the Alternative Nobel Prize in 2018. Her books have sold more than 850,000 copies around the world and have been translated into 29 languages and distributed across 40 countries and territories.

SHEILA FISCHMAN is the award-winning translator of some 200 contemporary novels from Quebec. In 2008 she was awarded the Molson Prize in the Arts. She is a Member of the Order of Canada and a chevalier of the Ordre national du Québec. She lives in Montreal.